GUNFIRE GAMBLE

The two gunmen had the girl in the cabin, and the edge on the Trailsman.

"Throw your damn gun in here," one of them called out to Fargo. "We'll give you ten seconds. Nine . . . eight . . . seven . . . six . . . five . . . four . . . three . . . two . . ."

"All right," Fargo shouted, and flung his Colt through the open doorway. Instantly he reached down and pulled his slender, double-edged throwing knife from his calf-holster.

"Walk in here with your hands up," one of the two called, and Skye obeyed.

It would be his knife against their bullets . . . his throwing arm against their trigger fingers . . . the worst odds he could think of, but the best ones he had. . . .

THE TRAILSMAN 90

MESABI HUNTDOWN

by

Jon Sharpe

A SIGNET BOOK

NEW AMERICAN LIBRARY

PUBLISHER'S NOTE

This book is a work of fiction. Names, characters, places, and incidents either are the product of the author's imagination or are used fictitiously, and any resemblance to actual persons, living or dead, events, or locales is entirely coincidental.

The first chapter of this book originally appeared in *Target Conestoga*, the eighty-ninth volume in this series.

SIGNET TRADEMARK REG. U.S. PAT. OFF. AND FOREIGN COUNTRIES
REGISTERED TRADEMARK—MARCA REGISTRADA
HECHO EN DRESDEN, TN, USA

SIGNET, SIGNET CLASSIC, MENTOR, ONYX, PLUME, MERIDIAN
and NAL BOOKS are published by NAL PENGUIN INC.,
1633 Broadway, New York, New York 10019

First Printing, June, 1989

1 2 3 4 5 6 7 8 9

PRINTED IN THE UNITED STATES OF AMERICA

The Trailsman

Beginnings . . . they bend the tree and they mark the man. Skye Fargo was born when he was eighteen. Terror was his midwife, vengeance his first cry. Killing spawned Skye Fargo, ruthless, cold-blooded murder. Out of the acrid smoke of gunpowder still hanging in the air, he rose, cried out a promise never forgotten.

The Trailsman they began to call him all across the West: searcher, scout, hunter, the man who could see where others only looked, his skills for hire but not his soul, the man who lived each day to the fullest, yet trailed each tomorrow. Skye Fargo, the Trailsman, the seeker who could take the wildness of a land and the wanting of a woman and make them his own.

Late August, 1859,
Northern Minnesota just below
the Rainy River at the
back edge of Crow country . . .

The lone horseman rode swiftly, his bronze-skinned, near-naked form glistening in the last of the day's sun. His black hair, heavy with fish oil, flowed back in the wind, held in place by a Crow headband. A short bow and a rawhide quiver of arrows were slung over his shoulder, a tomahawk tucked into the waistband of the breechclout he wore, his only garment of clothing. The sun began to drop over the horizon as he rode through stands of red cedar and hemlock, and the house came into view.

He rode down toward where the structure rose in the center of a small clearing. A road led to the clearing, but he came down from the low hills and saw the three guards on their horses at the edge of the treeline, each man carrying a rifle. They were, as they had been the day before, some thirty yards apart.

The bronze-skinned horseman moved the pinto to where the trees thinned and the three guards would see him. They reacted immediately, one bringing his gun around to fire off two hasty shots that went wild. The Crow warrior sent the pinto moving in and out of the trees. His narrowed eyes were on the house. He saw the door fly open and two more men rush out, both with revolvers in hand.

One of the three guards on horseback called out at once. "It's that goddamn Indian again," he said. "The one who was here yesterday."

"Forget him," one of the men who'd come from the house rasped. "He's not the one we have to look out for."

"He makes me nervous. What's he doing here?" the man on the horse answered.

"Maybe he's looking to steal some horses or maybe he just wants some coup stories to tell around the tribal fire," the other man said. "Kill him if he comes too close. Meanwhile, keep your eyes on that damned road." He turned, motioned to the man beside him, and both strode back into the house and pulled the door shut.

The Crow warrior turned his pinto and raced back in front of the three guards in the treeline, letting them glimpse him for the briefest of moments before disappearing back into the trees again. He halted suddenly to peer out at the horizon: the sun had vanished and dusk began to roll over the land and his eyes went to the house again. A grim smile broke the stonelike impassivity of his chiseled countenance. He had found out what he had wanted to learn. There were five guards, three outside the house and two inside. He waited, motionless, and let the dusk slide across the land while he watched the three outside guards position themselves again in the trees. They stayed on their horses, remaining some thirty yards apart, still visible in the lowering light of the day, each clearly able to watch the small road that led to the clearing and the house.

Before the light faded completely, the Crow warrior moved his pinto down closer to the three outside guards, again letting the animal crash through the brush as he raced along the line where the three men sat their horses. He allowed a fleeting glimpse of himself in the last of the light.

"It's that damn Indian again," he heard one of the men call out. He swerved the horse and disappeared deeper into the woods. He continued riding and let the sound of the horse's fast trot drift back to the three men until, out of hearing range, he halted and slid from the animal's back. He lowered himself to the ground, relaxed against a red cedar, and let the night grow deeper. Finally, he rose and began to move down the hillside on foot, the pinto following along behind him.

When he neared the line where the three outside guards waited, now shrouded in the blackness of the night, he halted and dropped the rope halter of the pinto over a branch, rested his hand against the horse's neck for a moment, and then moved on alone. On steps silent as a bobcat's prowl, he moved through the trees, each step firm yet feather-light as he passed through brush without rippling a twig and low branches without disturbing a leaf. Finally, the dark bulk of the nearest guard took shape atop his horse, and as the Crow drew nearer, he took a length of rawhide from the belt of his breechclout and twisted the thin strip in his hands.

The guard's attention was focused on the house and the road just below the slope where he waited, and he was totally unaware of the stealthy figure moving up behind him. But his horse picked up the presence of an intruder in the night, moved, pawed the ground, and snorted air restlessly. "Shut up and quiet down," the man growled in annoyance. "Damn-fool nag."

A wry smile touched the lips of the bronzed, near-naked figure. The damn fool sat in the saddle, he grunted silently. It was always the mark of a fool who didn't pay attention to his mount. But the stealthy figure moved forward and thanked the spirits for the number of such fools in the world.

When he was close enough, the horse still snorting air in alarm, the stealthy figure struck with a motion instant as a firefly's light and fluid as an arc of water.

11

In one motion, he sprang and looped the length of rawhide around the man's neck, and the man came out of the saddle without more than a faint, hissed gasp. The Crow caught the figure in midair and noiselessly lowered it to the ground. Unconscious, the man still breathed as the Crow pulled the length of rawhide away from his victim's throat. It would be at least ten minutes before enough oxygen returned to the man's brain to bring him out of unconsciousness.

The Indian hurried on, once again on swift, silent steps. The second guard came into sight under the light of the moon that filtered through the thick tree cover. He, too, had his gaze focused on the house and the road below.

The Crow warrior moved silently around to the front of the guard; his horse lifted its head, ears held straight as it picked up the Crow's scent. The powerful, bronze-skinned figure drew the bow from around his shoulders, placed an arrow on the string, and drew the bow back. When he suddenly rose up in front of the guard, the bow was drawn back as far as it would go, the arrow poised to take flight, and he saw the astonishment flood the man's face. It was the instant he had counted on, the numbing moment of surprise that froze the man in place, and when the man snapped himself out of his trance, the arrow was already hissing through the air.

The man reached for his revolver but he never got the weapon out of the holster as the arrow smashed into his chest, burying itself almost up to the feathers at that short range. The man grasped at the shaft protruding from his chest even as he toppled backward from his horse. His hands were still curled futilely around the shaft of the arrow as he hit the ground and lay still in one of the brushes.

There was one more, the warrior reminded himself as he moved through the forest. When he came to the third figure, he dropped to one knee. The man's attention was not riveted on the house or the road. He had plainly paid attention to the sudden restlessness of his horse and he turned in one direction and then another, peering into the dark of the surrounding trees. A shaft of moonlight caught the glint of the gun in his hand and the Crow's lips drew back in a grimace. Silence was still all-important. A shot would alert those inside the house.

But another arrow wasn't the answer. The guard was moving, and even if it did hit him full force, his finger might tighten on the trigger, and the shot would explode in the night like a cannon's roar. The near-naked figure stayed on one knee and waited, silent as a chuckwalla on a rock.

The guard finally stopped turning and brought his horse to a standstill facing the house. But the gun remained in his hand, and only when he finally pushed it into its holster did the Crow warrior rise to his feet. He moved closer to the guard and saw he'd have to come at the man from the side as a thick cluster of buckhorn plantain made any approach from behind impossible. He crept around the thick bushes, halted, measuring distance as he crouched and gathered every fiber of his powerful body. He leapt, a diving upward arc of his body, and the man in the saddle was struck by an arrow made of muscle, bone, and sinew. It smashed into his ribs and sent him flying from his horse. He hit the ground with a grunt of pain.

The Indian was upon him instantly, sinking one knee deep into the man's abdomen while he yanked the gun from its holster. He smashed the butt of the gun down onto the guard's skull, and the man lay still. The Crow rose, tossed the six-gun into the bushes, and turned toward the house in the clearing. Lamplight burned in two of the rooms, the larger in the front of the house and a smaller window near the back. He saw one of the guards move past the window in the large room and brought his gaze to the other room. The young woman finally appeared for a moment and then moved out of sight. The Crow warrior darted from the trees to cut across the cleared land around the house. He spied the door at the rear of the building and was at it in half-a-dozen long strides.

He closed his hand around the doorknob and the door came open. He slipped into the house to pause inside a dimly lighted corridor. A lamp burned at the far end of the hallway and he heard the two men talking somewhere around the corner of the hall. He turned and moved on silent steps down to the other end of the corridor to find the room where he had seen the young woman. He'd take her from under their noses in silence if he could, he told himself, and he quickly found the room, the only one with a sliver of light coming from under the door. Once again he closed his hand on a doorknob and turned it ever so slowly until the latch came open so softly even he couldn't hear it.

The young woman sat at a small table at the side of the room, brushing her hair in front of a mirror. The brown hair hung shoulder-length, a fine, gossamer texture to it. Clad only in a white nightgown of a material that fairly shimmered in the lamplight, she had broad, square shoulders and a long waist that widened into full hips. He crossed the room with soundless steps and the young woman didn't know he was there until the reflection of the smooth, powerfully muscled chest suddenly appeared in the mirror.

He saw her stare at the reflection, uncertain whether she was seeing or imagining, and she suddenly spun on the stool to peer at him. Astonishment and terror welled up in her eyes; her lips, red and full, fell open; and the scream began to gather in her throat. The Crow warrior brought his fist downward in a short, clipping blow that landed alongside her jaw. Her eyes

14

rolled back into her head at once and she collapsed as he caught her before she hit the floor.

He lowered her to the floor and glimpsed full, up-turned breasts that partly spilled from one side of the nightgown. He took another moment to scan the room, and he pulled a handful of garments from a closet that was partly open and tossed them into a canvas sack near the bed that took up part of the room. With a quick, almost effortless motion, he scooped the young woman from the floor and tossed her over one shoulder. The sack in his hand, he fled the room and felt the warm softness of her stomach against his shoulder and the smooth roundness of her rear as he held her in place with one hand. He had almost reached the back door when he heard the shout. He whirled to see one of the two guards had stepped into the corridor.

"Holy Jesus," the man shouted. "It's the goddamn Indian."

The warrior pulled the door open and fled outside as he saw the man yank a six-gun from its holster. He heard the shot splinter the door behind him as he ran into the open, and he knew the guard would charge from the house, six-gun blazing, before he could cross the clear space to the trees. He dropped to one knee against the outer wall of the house and let the girl slide to the ground and had the tomahawk in hand, his arm raised, as the guard burst from the back door. The man halted for an instant as he frowned, his gaze sweeping the cleared land where he had plainly expected to see the fleeing figure. Before he had a chance to turn, the tomahawk smashed into the side of his face, imbedding itself almost to the handle. The man toppled with the front and back of his head almost two halves.

The second guard was following quickly, the Indian realized, and he was racing in a crouch toward the door when the man ran from the house. The second guard halted and stared for a moment at the crumpled figure on the ground, and then, catching the sound of racing footsteps, he whirled, firing as he did. But the Crow had already dived, a low, downward tackle that caught the last guard just below the knees as he felt the bullets pass over his back.

The man went down, still firing, his shots going harmlessly into the air. The warrior reached one long, muscled arm out and caught the man's wrist. He bent it backward and the guard dropped the gun with a curse of pain. But he managed to bring his knee up and sink it into the Indian's abdomen. The Crow fell back for an instant, his grip on the man's wrist coming loose. The guard whirled on the ground, trying to reach his gun. But the big, bronzed figure smashed a fist down on the back of his head. The blow drove the man's face into the ground, and when he tried to lift his head, the Indian seized him by the hair, half-lifted and half-turned him, and smashed a thundering blow into his face. The man fell forward and lay still as the Crow let go of his hair.

He'd be unconscious for more than long enough, the Indian grunted as he returned to the girl, lifted her over his shoulder again, and scooped up the sack of clothes. He moved calmly and quietly into the trees and made his way back to where he'd left the pinto. He placed the girl across the horse's back on her stomach, held the sack by its strap, and climbed onto the horse. He undid the rope halter from the branch and moved unhurriedly away. He rode north through the trees and kept the young woman in place with one hand. He had left the slope, crossed a low ridge, and moved on when the young woman awoke and he saw her try to lift her head to look up at him. Not ungently, yet firmly, he pushed her head down with one hand and continued to ride northward.

"I'm getting an upset stomach," he heard the girl

say. "Not that you'd understand or give a damn." He rode on and she fell silent and stayed that way except for an occasional oath of discomfort. He had reached open land before he drew to a halt at the edge of a small lake where a crack willow grew to the very shore in front of a tall stand of pokeweed. He patted the young woman on her round, firm rear; she slid from the horse, landed on her feet, and watched him dismount. He motioned to the ground and she lowered herself onto a bed of elf's-cap moss, and he glimpsed the combination of fear and defiance in her eyes as he turned his back to her.

He walked to the lake and stepped into the water, glanced back, and saw surprise add itself to the emotions mirrored in her eyes. The Crow warrior immersed himself in the water, executed a quick dive under the surface, and came up shaking a cascade of water from himself. He dived again, surfaced, rolled twice in the water, and swam the few yards to the shore. He rose from the water, walked onto the shoreline, every bit as beautifully muscled, but the bronze sheen to his skin had been replaced by a deep tan. The browband gone, his hair, while still black, was no longer flat and heavy with fish oil and fell in a soft wave. The young woman stared at him and, for the first time, saw the lake blue of his eyes.

"Damn. You're no Indian," she breathed.

"Go to the head of the class," the big man said.

She stared, her frown of astonishment deepening with each passing moment. "You're him," she breathed. "The one they expected."

"I figured they might be expecting somebody," the big man said.

Her eyes narrowed ever so slightly. "Why'd you expect that?" she asked.

"Your Uncle Cyrus isn't the kind to keep anything

quiet. I knew he'd brag and men are quick to sell information," the big man answered.

Her lips pursed in thought for a moment. "So you came as an Indian," she murmured.

"It let me get close enough to see, count noses, and find out what I wanted to know," he said.

"And they'd dismiss you as an Indian looking to steal some horses, maybe," she finished. "Very clever. You've a real name, I presume."

"Fargo . . . Skye Fargo. Some call me the Trailsman," the big man said. He let his gaze take in the young woman properly for the first time. Tall, slightly longish breasts, but with nicely upturned cups that pressed two tiny points into the silk of the nightgown. A narrow and long waist and long thighs under the gown. She had fine, gossamerlike brown hair in an even-featured face: full red lips, a short nose, and eyes so light brown they were almost beige. She was damned attractive, he decided, yet there was an edge of hardness in her face, a mirror of something inside. "No need for me to ask your name. You're Julie Hudson," Fargo said, and she answered with a half-smile. "Where's your stepfather?" he questioned.

"Away for a few days," the young woman said.

"We won't be waiting," Fargo said, and walked to the thick cluster of pokeweed, reached in, and drew out a bundle of clothes, then a saddle and a bedroll. "I'm going to get some sleep," he said.

"Like that?" Julie Hudson asked, eyes flicking to the wet breechclout he still wore as his only clothing.

"Why not? It's easy to get used to and it makes for comfortable sleeping." Fargo laughed. "You can sleep on the moss or I'll give you a blanket."

"The moss. It's a warm night," she said, and he saw her frown as she watched him take the lariat from around the saddle horn and walk toward her with it. "What's that for?"

18

"So's I can get some sleep without worrying about you," Fargo said. "You see, maybe you don't mind going back to your uncle, but maybe you do. He never made that clear."

"What if I told you I wouldn't try to run?" Julie Hudson asked.

Fargo smiled affably. "Wouldn't make any difference, honey," he said.

Her beige eyes held him in a studied glance. "You don't take any chances, do you?" she commented.

"No more than I have to." Fargo smiled and looped the lariat around her left wrist and then tied the other end around his. He walked some ten feet away from her and stretched out on the soft moss. "I'm a very light sleeper," he said, the pleasant matter-of-fact tone a thin disguise for the warning in his words. He watched the young woman settle herself on the moss, her movements smoothly graceful, and she lay down with her back toward him.

"Good night," she murmured, and he grunted a reply with his eyes closed.

The soft lapping of the water against the shore was a soothing sound that brought sleep quickly.

Fargo stayed asleep through the night, waking only when he felt a tug at his wrist but saw it was only the girl turning onto her back. When he woke with the first rays of the dawn sun, Julie Hudson still slept, the silk nightgown up high enough to reveal a long, lovely calf.

Fargo rose, untied the rope around his wrist, and took off the breechclout. He stuffed it into the bottom of his saddlebag and washed with the lake water before donning trousers and gun belt. The girl still lay asleep, so he sat down near the water, leaned back on his elbows, and let thoughts drift back to the events that had brought him here.

Cyrus Reiber had come to him after he'd completed

a trailblazing drive for Ted Wilks from Dodge City up to the South Dakota Territory through too much Sioux country. "I'm told you're the very best and I need the very best," Cyrus Reiber had told him at their first meeting in a saloon just over the border in Minnesota Territory. He had run a hand through thinning brown hair and offered the kind of money only a fool would turn down. "Meet me at Rock Table in a week and I'll give you the details," Reiber had said. "That's just below Rainy River."

"A week." Fargo had nodded and pocketed the money. He'd taken his time and relaxed on the ride north through Minnesota and found Cyrus Reiber waiting for him at the saloon in Rock Table. The man had consumed one or two whiskeys while waiting and his somewhat bulbous nose had taken on the red flush of veins long accustomed to alcohol. Cyrus Reiber, medium height, thin of build, had a garrulous quality to him that made him take a spell before he got into the heart of what he had in his mind. Fargo patiently let the man order another round of drinks.

"It's my niece, Julie Hudson," Cyrus Reiber finally said between sips of whiskey. "I want you to get her and bring her back to me."

"Why?" Fargo asked crisply.

"Because she's supposed to be with me," Cyrus Reiber said with some indignation.

"Why?" Fargo repeated, unfazed by the man's reaction.

"Because her real pa left instructions that I was to take care of Julie if anything happened to her ma," Cyrus Reiber said.

"Where is she now?" Fargo had asked.

"Her stepfather, Tom Colson, has her," the man said.

"Maybe you'd better start at the beginning," Fargo

suggested, and Cyrus Reiber sat back after downing his drink.

"Julie Hudson's real pa died when she was about seven or eight years old. This Tom Colson came along and married her ma, and Julie lived with them. Colson's a no-good four-flusher, but I didn't make a fuss. I thought it was best for Julie to stay with her ma, but I kept an eye on her," Cyrus said. "But when her ma died two years ago, Colson refused to let me take over Julie. He kept moving from place to place with her. God knows what he's filled her head with about me. But I paid a lot of money for information and I know where he has her now. I want you to bring her back to me. It's what her real pa, Frank Hudson, said he wanted to happen."

Fargo had listened carefully, turned Cyrus Reiber's words in his mind. "You know where she is. Doesn't seem you need a trailsman to get her."

"She'll be under guard. Only a man with your skills can get to her. But that's only the first part. After you get her, there'll be plenty more that sure as hell will need a trailsman," Cyrus Reiber had answered. "That's why I'm paying you the kind of money I am."

Fargo recalled how he had nodded agreement and had set out on the first leg of his task. He recalled how he'd kept thinking of Reiber's whiskey-inspired loquaciousness and knew it was more than likely he'd bragged about hiring someone to get his niece back. It was that certainty that had led him to disguise himself as a Crow warrior. He was glad for it now. They had definitely been expecting him and he snapped thoughts off as the young woman woke and rubbed sleep from her eyes as she sat up.

In the first, relaxed, unwary moments of waking, she seemed softer, the hard edge gone from her face. "Get dressed. We've riding to do," Fargo said.

"I'd like to wash in the lake first," she said.

"Be my guest," Fargo said.

"Not with an audience," she snapped.

"I'm not an audience," Fargo said chidingly. "Your Uncle Cyrus sent me to fetch you, remember?"

"He didn't send you to ogle," she returned tartly.

He shrugged. "It's against my principles not to look," Fargo insisted.

"What principles?" she half-sneered.

"One of them is never turn your back on beauty," he said, and smiled pleasantly.

"Thanks for the compliment," she said.

"Don't mention it," he said cheerfully.

"Nevertheless, make an exception this time," she said firmly.

He shrugged again. "This time," he said, and turned away. He heard her go into the lake, and when he looked again, she was swimming and turning in the water and he caught a glimpse of long legs and graceful movements. He took a towel from his saddlebag and tossed it on the shore and turned his attention to saddling the Ovaro.

She finally emerged, dried herself, and dressed. When he finished tightening the cinch, he turned and saw her in a black skirt and a yellow shirt, looking very attractive, but the edge of hardness had returned to her face.

He motioned to the magnificent Ovaro with the jet-black front and hind quarters and the gleaming white midsection, and she climbed into the saddle. She sat very straight as he swung up behind her, but a firm yet soft rear nonetheless pressed against his legs.

"I prefer riding this way," she commented, and he laughed.

"Tell me about your Uncle Cyrus. What's he got against your stepfather?" Fargo asked as he sent the pinto northward across Minnesota Territory.

"I don't really know. I guess he thinks Tom's not a good influence for me," she said.

"That true?" Fargo queried.

She shrugged. "I don't know."

"He's been living with your ma and you for a long time. You've got to have some idea on that," Fargo pressed.

"He was away a lot," the young woman said.

Fargo felt the small furrow cross his brow as he pushed another remark at Julie Hudson. "Cyrus told me he kept an eye on you over the years," he said.

"I guess you could say that," she answered, and Fargo felt the furrow dig deeper. She'd given him only bland, careful answers on everything he'd asked, almost as though she feared to say anything more. He broke off asking her further questions and spurred the Ovaro through the gently rolling hillsides until he stopped at another small lake to let the horse rest.

Julie Hudson sat down at the water's edge, cooled her wrists in the water, and finally leaned back on her elbows and let her eyes sweep the terrain. "It's nice here. I like all these lakes. They're all so blue and pure."

"That's why the Indians named this land Minnesota," Fargo said. "That means the place where the sky is in the land."

She smiled, her longish breasts moving gracefully as she half-turned on one side, her long waist and long legs adding to the smoothness of her every movement.

"Guess you haven't lived long in Minnesota Territory," Fargo remarked.

"We moved around a lot," she said, and he smiled inwardly. It was there again, the answers that were not really answers, never a definite reply.

"Time to ride," he said cheerfully, and she came to her feet with a fluid smoothness that was pretty to see. He set a faster pace when he rode on and he reached

Cyrus Reiber's house just before the sun began to dip down over the horizon. The man came hurrying out of the front door of his small house as Fargo rode to a halt and swung from the Ovaro.

The girl stayed in the saddle and Fargo gestured to her as he smiled. "One niece, signed, sealed, and delivered," he said. "Though it took a little doing."

Cyrus Reiber's eyes stayed fixed on the young woman. "She's not my niece," he said. "She's not Julie."

2

Fargo let the man's words revolve inside him as he stared at Cyrus Reiber. "What do you mean, she's not your niece?" He frowned.

"Just what I said. That's not Julie Hudson," the man said, his bulbous nose seeming to expand.

"Dammit, she was the one there, waiting in her bedroom," Fargo snapped.

"I don't care where she was. This isn't Julie. I never saw this girl in my life," Cyrus Reiber snapped back.

Fargo turned his lake-blue eyes on the young woman and felt the iciness creeping through his body. She glanced back at him with a veil over her beige eyes. "You want to start explaining?" he growled.

She shrugged and her face remained composed. "Explain about what?" she asked.

"You know goddamn well what!" Fargo exploded. "The man says you're not his niece. Then who the hell are you?"

"Julie Hudson," the girl said.

"Goddamn, she's lying," Cyrus Reiber shouted, and Fargo saw the red creeping up over his collar and into his face.

"Talk," Fargo said to the girl. "No more lying."

"How do you know he's not the one lying?" she said calmly, and Fargo tossed another glance at Cyrus Reiber and saw the man's cheeks quivering in indignation. He returned his eyes to the girl.

"He's not that good an actor," Fargo said. "Now, you want to talk or sit in a jail cell?"

"For what?" the girl asked.

Cyrus Reiber's voice broke in. "For posin' as somebody you're not. For maybe putting my niece in danger. Sheriff McKay's a friend of mine. He'll hold you in jail till your hair turns gray, young woman," he said.

Fargo saw a flash of apprehension in the girl's beige eyes and she let a dissatisfied expression touch her lips. "I can't sit in jail. I've someplace to be," she muttered half to herself.

"Then start talking," Fargo said. "Who the hell are you and why'd you pose as Julie Hudson?"

The girl gave a shrug. "All right, I've done enough. I'll talk, but not here. I'm thirsty and hot."

"Bring her into the house," Cyrus Reiber said.

Fargo's hand closed around the girl's elbow and she made no move to pull away. He took her inside the house; the living room was modestly furnished, with wallpaper badly in need of replacing. The older man disappeared into the kitchen and returned with a glass of water for the girl, and after she drank most of it, she set it on an end table.

"You were hired to stand in as Julie Hudson," Fargo said. "Who hired you?"

"Tom Colson," she said.

"That rotten bastard," Cyrus Reiber interjected.

"He expected somebody would be coming for Julie," Fargo offered, and the girl nodded. He turned a cold gaze on Cyrus Reiber. "Now how'd they come to expect that?" he questioned.

"Guess he just figured I'd be sending somebody for her," Reiber said with a shrug.

"Not good enough," Fargo growled. "How many people did you talk to over a bottle?"

The man had the grace to look uncomfortable. "A

few, maybe. Told them I was getting my niece back,"
he muttered.

"Figured that'd happen," Fargo said, his voice harsh,
and turned back to the girl. "What's your name?" he
asked.

"Denise Farr."

"Was Julie Hudson there when you arrived?" Fargo
asked.

"I didn't see her."

"He took off with her and left you, to buy time,"
Fargo thought aloud. "You know why?"

"No. All I know is what I was hired to do," Denise
said.

Fargo took in the reply with reservations. "Why
didn't you tell me when we were on our way here?" he
questioned.

"I was hired to keep it going as long as I could,"
Denise said.

"You did your job well," Fargo conceded.

"So did you. I was scared as hell when I thought a
damn Crow brave had me," she said, and then a slow,
reflective smile slid across her full red lips. "But you
weren't who I thought you were and I wasn't who you
thought I was. Kind of poetic justice, wasn't it?"

"Poetic justice, hell," Reiber burst in again. "Julie's
in danger and you put her there."

"I didn't put anybody anywhere. I was hired to do a
job and I did it," Denise shot back.

"Damn your hide," the man spat, and spun on
Fargo. "I'm doubling my pay to you. I want you to go
after them, find them, and get Julie away from Tom
Colson."

Fargo's lips pursed as he considered the man's offer.
There were a lot of aspects that didn't fit right. "Why
would Tom Colson run off with her?" he asked.

"There's land and money in our family. Julie is his
ticket into family affairs. While she's in his hands, he

27

can get her to do what he wants. He can manipulate and maneuver her. She's young and trusting."

"Why is it so important for you to have her?" Fargo pressed.

"I'm her real kin," the man said with some indignation. "I'll protect her from wheeling, dealing four-flushers like Tom Colson. Besides, her pa wanted me to take care of her."

Fargo let thoughts dance inside his head. Reiber's answers held more anger and self-righteousness than his explanation accounted for. There was something else. Everyone seemed to be going to an awful lot of trouble over Julie Hudson: a decoy hired and set up, a flight that might or might not be a kidnapping, and a desperate urgency to Cyrus Reiber's desire to have the girl in his hands. The explanations he offered were too ordinary for all that, Fargo mused. But the money was too good to turn down. And he'd been duped. That always stuck hard inside him.

"All right, I'll get her for you," he said. Satisfaction flashed in Reiber's veined and bloodshot face. Fargo turned to Denise. "What about her?" he asked.

"Let her go her way. She's no good to us," Reiber said.

Without agreeing with the man's opinion, Fargo nodded and started to walk from the house. "I'll be leaving now. I'll have to try to pick up a trail, come morning."

"Time's important, Fargo," the man said. "There's no telling what a man like Tom Colson might do."

Fargo nodded and strode outside to see the sun starting to dip down beyond the horizon as he swung onto the Ovaro. "Just you wait a damn minute," he heard the voice call and saw Denise Farr hurrying after him, longish breasts swaying from side to side. "I need a horse. You can get me one or the money to buy one," the young woman said.

"You've your brass, girl." Fargo frowned at her. "I've no call to get you a damn thing."

"Yes you do," she insisted, and managed to sound righteous. "I was doing my job. You come in, knock me out, and carry me off. You didn't even give me a chance to take my money."

"Didn't figure you'd need any," Fargo said. "I didn't know you'd turn out to be a damn fraud."

"No matter, it still leaves me without a horse or money. Now, you get me a horse or take me to Rock Table," Denise said stubbornly.

"What happens there?" Fargo asked.

"I'll get money enough to buy me a horse," she said.

Fargo met her defiant glower. Her words held a measure of truth, and the idea of leaving her stranded, penniless, and on foot in this untamed country didn't sit well with him. Besides, he was certain she knew more than she'd said, maybe more than she realized. He let himself utter a deep sigh.

"I always did have a conscience," he said. "I'll make you a deal. You answer my questions and I'll take you to Rock Table."

"It's a deal," she said quickly.

He reached down and pulled her onto the horse in front of him. His arms pressed against the sides of her breasts as he held the reins and moved the Ovaro forward.

"How come Tom Colson picked you to stand in for Julie Hudson?" he asked as he sent the horse downhill.

"No special reason. He was looking for somebody and I happened to be in the right place," Denise said.

"Which was?"

"Waiting tables in a dance hall in Reelfoot, on the Tennessee-Kentucky border," Denise said. "He told me what he wanted and offered more money than I'd make in a year waiting tables. I took the job."

"He say anything when he brought you to his place?"

"Only what I was supposed to do."

"And you never saw Julie Hudson."

"I told you that already," she bristled.

"Hold your damn temper," Fargo growled.

She half-turned in the saddle to look at him, her face suddenly softened with a rush of concern. "Look, I didn't know I'd be getting anybody in trouble when I took the job. Colson made it sound like it was some kind of joke."

Fargo nodded and let some of the hardness leave his eyes. She was tough in the ways of those who've learned about people and life the hard way. Yet the toughness hadn't turned into bitter hardness yet. That undercurrent of softness was still part of her. "How long did Tom Colson stay around after he brought you there?" Fargo questioned.

"A week or so," the girl said.

"That means he'd already stashed Julie Hudson away someplace and was only out to buy more time," Fargo thought aloud. "He try to be especially nice to you?" he questioned.

"No," Denise snapped. She peered again at his chiseled handsomeness. "You try from all angles, don't you?"

"That's how you learn things," Fargo answered. Not that he had learned anything, he grunted silently. Yet he was certain Denise knew more than she'd told him. He broke off speculation as he saw the dark outline of the town appear on the horizon as the dusk began to become night. "How do you figure to get money in Rock Table?" he asked.

"That's none of your concern," she answered stiffly. She turned around to peer at him again, and her beige eyes were darkened. "Not by peddling my ass, if that's what you're thinking."

He smiled. "No, I didn't figure you for that."

Her frown held. "Meaning I couldn't or I wouldn't?"

"Damn, you're hard-nosed." Fargo grinned. "Some of both. You've too much sass to sell it and too much brass to give it away."

She smoothed her frown away. "That might be a compliment. I'll think about it," she murmured.

He laughed and put the Ovaro into a trot as darkness descended. The night had cloaked Rock Table when he rode into town and halted in the center of Main Street.

Denise slid from the saddle and gazed up at him. "Thanks for the ride, Fargo," she said, her eyes on him with a long, thoughtful look, and a slow smile came to edge her full lips. "Maybe we'll meet again, a different way and a different time. It might be good."

"It might be," Fargo agreed. She had her own brand of appealingness, her hard-bitten exterior with a tough yet real inner integrity. She had accepted the world on its own harsh terms without compromising with it. "Take care of yourself, honey," he said.

"You, too, Fargo," she said, and he watched her walk down the dark street. Her long waist moved gracefully, her tight, slender rear hardly caused a ripple in the skirt.

He turned the Ovaro into the narrow space between two buildings and dismounted at once to hurry outside on foot in time to see her disappearing along Main Street. He followed, stayed tight against the buildings where the shadows were deepest. He still felt certain that Denise knew more than she had said, but he was definitely convinced she had someone to meet in Rock Table. If it were Tom Colson, he intended to join the party. He quickened his pace as the slender figure continued to march down the street.

Denise passed the dance hall and was illuminated for a moment in the shaft of light that reached out from the open doors. Fargo slowed until she went on into the darkness again. She was nearly at the end of town when she halted at a ramshackle structure. The faded letters on the wall proclaimed it had once been a saddlery shop. A light-brown horse switched its tail beside a hitching rail outside, and Fargo halted, watched as she knocked at the door. A lamp went on inside and Fargo saw the door opened and a man appear, one hand on his six-gun.

"Well, now, this is a nice surprise," he rasped.

"Willie Maxim?" Denise asked.

"That's me," the man said, and Fargo took in a medium-sized figure, a sharp-nosed face with deep cheek lines and a smile that was more of a sneer than anything else. "Shit, you must be the one Colson hired," the man said, staring at Denise.

"He said you'd have the rest of my money. He only paid me half," Denise said.

"Yeah, sure, come on in," the man said. He held the door open for Denise to enter.

When he pulled it shut after her, Fargo crossed to the house in a half-dozen long-legged strides to peer through the lone window caked with years of dirt. He could see only smudged figures inside but the cracked and splintered walls let him hear clearly.

"Colson said you might never show up," the man said.

"Why wouldn't I show up? I only got half the money he promised me," Denise said.

"Well, you won't be collecting it here, sweetie," the man said.

"Why not?" Denise asked, anger gathering in her voice. "Did you spend it?"

"Maybe I did and maybe he never left it. Don't you worry about it, girlie. You got half. Be happy and git," the man said, a rasp in his tone.

"The hell I will. You give me the rest of my money," Denise snapped.

Fargo, peering hard through the caked windowpane, saw the man's figure move, one arm shoot out to seize Denise by the hair. She gave a short cry of pain as he yanked her forward. "I'll give you somethin' better, girlie," Fargo heard him snarl, and he saw Denise twist and her leg come up and out. "Ow, Jesus," he heard the man cry in pain. He doubled over as Denise tore from his grasp.

On one knee, holding his groin with one hand, the man flung out curses, but Fargo saw the smudged figure of Denise whirl, reach out, and grab hold of something that turned out to be a shovel. She started to swing it at the man when he rose, moved backward, and yanked his gun out.

"Goddamn bitch, I'll shoot your damn head off." Denise halted and lowered the shovel to the ground. "Get on the floor, on your stomach," Maxim ordered.

Fargo moved from the window. The Colt in his hand, he yanked the door open and saw the man, standing over Denise, look up in surprise. "Drop the gun," Fargo said.

"Who the hell are you?" Maxim frowned, the gun still pointed down at Denise, though his eyes were on the big man in the doorway.

"Drop the gun first," Fargo said, his eyes focused on the man's gun hand and wrist. It allowed him the split-second warning that Willie Maxim decided to be stupid, that instant that spelled the difference between life and death. The man's wrist moved as he started to bring his gun hand up, and Fargo's finger tightened on the trigger of the big Colt. Maxim took the heavy shell full in the chest and flew backward as a shower of red cascaded into the air. He landed in a heap against the wall as Denise pushed to her feet and ran to press herself against Fargo.

"Thanks," she breathed, both hands pressed into his arm.

33

Fargo stared grimly at the collapsed figure against the wall, his jaw throbbing. "Damn fool," he muttered. Finally he brought his eyes to Denise.

"You followed me," she said.

"No kidding," he grunted.

"Why?"

"You were so anxious to get to Rock Table. I figured it wasn't to go sightseeing."

Her lips tightened in grudging admission and she turned to the figure on the floor. "I don't know if Tom Colson ever left him my money or he spent it, but I know I don't have it," she said. "I also know I'm going to get it, dammit."

"Maybe you ought to just forget about it," Fargo suggested.

Instant indignation flooded her face. "Hell, no. I earned it. It was my pay. I'm going to get it."

"Let's get out of here," Fargo said.

"Wait." Denise strode to the crumpled figure, knelt down, and began to go through the man's pockets, a grimace of distaste on her face. Finally she pulled out a handful of bills. "Twelve dollars," she counted, and pushed to her feet. "This'll have to do for now."

"You are one real little hard-nose, aren't you?" Fargo said with a certain grudging admiration.

"I didn't like doing that, but this'll buy me a horse tomorrow," Denise said.

"You don't need a horse. You can ride his. He won't be using it," Fargo told her as he left the shack with her.

"I guess that's true enough." Denise frowned. "But I'm not using his saddle. I'll buy my own tomorrow." Outside, she went to the horse and rummaged through the saddlebag. But she didn't find any more money so she finally climbed onto the light-brown steed. "I'll use his saddle as a trade-in, come tomorrow," she said.

"Where are you going to bed down?" Fargo asked.

"I don't know. Someplace not too far from town," she said.

"I'll find us a spot," he said, and she followed as he sent the Ovaro up a gentle hill and finally found a low-branched, spreading yellow poplar set back in a cluster of trees. He dismounted and took a blanket from his saddlebag and spread it on the ground. "This'll do fine," he said. "I've some dried-beef strips we can share."

"Thanks," she said, and sat down to eat hungrily. Finally, finished, she relaxed and leaned back on her elbows.

The pale moonlight trickled through the tree and Fargo was surprised at the softness that came over her. "What's Denise Farr been doing most of her life?"

"Knocking around. My folks died when I was fifteen. I'd no close kin, to I was on my own. I listened, watched, learned, made my own way. It hasn't been easy but it's been fun sometimes," she said.

"Nobody come to carry you off? You're right pretty beneath all that hard-nosed brass," Fargo said.

"There was a man once, a good man. I was getting ready to go off with him when he got himself killed standing too close to a shoot-out." A moment of pensiveness passed over her face.

"Sorry," Fargo said, and she nodded and shook away old thoughts.

"I learned it's a hard world, even when you least expect it," Denise said, the tightness returning to her face at once. She rose, took her canvas sack, and started for the high brush.

"I was hoping all that modesty was only playacting as Julie Hudson." Fargo smiled.

She tossed a glance back. "Some of it was, but I'm not about to put on a show, either," she said, and disappeared into the blackness. He undressed down to his underdrawers and was stretched out on the blanket when she returned. She sat down on one edge of the blanket in the nightgown and he saw her eyes move across the beautiful symmetry of his muscled frame. "I guess I'm lucky you decided to follow me," she murmured.

"I'd say so." He put his hands behind his head, closed his eyes, and began to wait for sleep. He heard her move, opened his eyes just in time to see her face over his and then her full red lips were pressing against his mouth, gently soft, and his hands came up to encircle her back. But she pulled away, half-rolled, and returned to her part of the blanket. "What was that for?" he asked.

"A thank you."

"Just once?"

"Saying thank you is once. More would be something else," she said. "Good night."

Hard-nose, he grunted silently, but he smiled as he closed his eyes again and drew sleep to himself.

The night stayed quiet and he slept well to wake with the warm morning sun. Denise sat up, rubbed sleep from her eyes, and he handed her his canteen. "Use this," he said. She rose, disappeared into the brush, and returned dressed, her face scrubbed to glistening, her fine, gossamer brown hair falling attractively to one side of her face.

"I'll be going into town for that saddle," she said. "Wait for me. I won't be long."

"Sorry, honey. Time's important. I've got to go all the way back to where I found you and try to pick up a trail," he said.

"No you don't," she said, and pulled herself onto the horse.

Frowning, Fargo reached out and took hold of the horse's cheek strap. "What does that mean?"

"Let me get a saddle first," she said, and he saw the hard-nosed stubbornness come into her face. He swore under his breath but released his hold on the cheek strap.

"Be quick about it," he growled, and watched her hurry off. He sat down under the tree and relaxed, though not happily. She obviously was still holding out, playing her own game her own way. But maybe it was worth waiting to find out more, he told himself. A little more than an hour had passed when Denise rode into sight and he was on his feet when she reached him. He took in a saddle with fancy metal studs along the edge of the skirt. "Going to a Mexican fiesta?" he murmured.

"It was the best buy," she retorted.

He fastened her with a cold stare. "You're here. Talk," Fargo growled. "You're still holding out, it seems."

"I know where the rest of my money might be."

"Along with Tom Colson and Julie Hudson?"

She shrugged. "I can't say to that. Maybe and maybe not. But there was a place I heard him talk to his men about."

"Where?" Fargo barked.

"I'll tell you if you promise to take me there."

"Another deal?"

"You could call it that, I guess," Denise said with defiance in her beige eyes.

"Someday you're going to deal yourself into big trouble, honey."

"Maybe, but that'll be my problem then. Right now, that's the deal. You take me and I'll save you days of time and trouble."

"I'll take you," Fargo growled.

"Colson talked to his men about a place at Crane Lake," Denise said. "He told the ones he left at the house to go there after I was taken off."

37

Fargo frowned and thought aloud. It was a lead, a lot more than he had without it. "Crane Lake's down south along the Rainy River," he muttered. "We'd do best to go to Lake Rainy and follow it down. Let's ride."

He turned the Ovaro and set out across the top of the hill. They headed east in a steady, ground-consuming pace. Fargo rode in silence and Denise stayed alongside or a half-pace behind until he halted beside a wide stream after the day had gone well past the noon hour.

"You're awfully quiet," Denise commented, a question curled inside the remark.

"I'm always quiet when I'm wondering."

"Wondering what?"

"What else you're holding out on me," he said. Her lips tightened but she made no reply. He took his shirt off and rubbed his chest and arms with the cool spring water, refilled his canteen and waited while Denise knelt beside the stream. He enjoyed her long-waisted grace as she leaned forward, opened her shirt buttons enough to remain modest while rubbing the cool water into the hollow between her breasts. But he managed to enjoy a glimpse of long, cream-white curves that rose up from lovely fullness, and when she finished and buttoned up again, he was in the saddle. She climbed onto her horse and he started forward through the heavily forested countryside.

"Most people don't do what they say they will. They just use you and toss you away," Denise suddenly blurted out belligerently. The words seemed to be pulled out of midair but they had been simmering inside her. Fargo turned a cool glance at her. "I've learned that," she added defensively.

"So you hold out."

"I protect myself."

"Why tell me about it? Feeling guilty?"

"Absolutely not," she returned. "I was trying to explain, that's all."

"Thanks," Fargo said laconically, and she returned a tight-lipped glare. He didn't pursue the subject and concentrated on moving down into as many valleys as he could find rather than tire the horses with hill riding. He saw the night coming when he cut around International Falls and increased the pace as he made straight for the western edge of Rainy Lake. When he reached a place where the trees thinned and the land opened up more, he drew the big Sharps from its saddle holster and slowed as he scanned the brush. He had caught the movement in two different places already, and now, rifle in hand, he was ready when he spotted the quick, upward flurry of flight that was the mark of the ruffed grouse. Three of the birds took off with their whirred beating of wings, almost straight into the air. He swung the rifle, fired, and a grouse plummeted to the ground. "Supper," he said, and rode off to retrieve the bird.

When he returned to Denise, he turned east again. She followed until, as the purple gray of twilight began to descend, he reached the shore of the long, irregularly shaped lake. He pulled up under the leaves of a black willow that grew almost to the water's edge. While Denise gathered firewood, he plucked the grouse, singed the pinfeathers, and with a makeshift spit set the bird to roasting as night descended. A nearly full moon rose to paint a silver path across the quiet waters of Lake Rainy, and the night grew still. The bird roasted quickly, and after they ate, Denise sat back on her elbows and Fargo watched the moonlight outline the upward, lovely curve of her breasts.

"This is a beautiful spot," she observed.

"Perfect for romance, I'd say," Fargo ventured.

"I'm sure you would," Denise said with a touch of asperity. He leaned back and stared out across the silver-touched lake as thoughts lazily slid across his mind. "What are you thinking about?" Denise asked after a long while.

"Julie Hudson," Fargo said. "I'm thinking there's an awful lot of fuss and feathers over her."

"Meaning what exactly?"

"Things don't fit right, starting with Cyrus Reiber. He wants to protect her awful bad, too damn bad," Fargo muttered. "And her stepfather's too hell-bent on keeping her to himself just for a ticket into the family."

"You saying Reiber's lied to you about himself and about Colson?"

"I'm saying it's damn possible. I smell something more. I don't know what it is, but there's something," Fargo said.

She took his words in and said nothing more and he finally rose, put out the fire, and turned to her. "Time to get some shut-eye," he said, and she took her sack, marched around to the other side of the tree, and reappeared in the nightgown. He had undressed and was stretched out on the blanket as she sat down on one corner and studied him for a long moment.

"You're right," she said, and drew a frown from him. "About Julie Hudson. There is something more to it."

He sat up and peered at her. "What do you know?"

"Not anything real, but I overheard Tom Colson talking to some of his men. You're right, he wants her for more than a ticket into family affairs. He kept talking about her being his way to becoming a rich man," Denise said.

"You hear anything else?" Fargo questioned.

"No more than that," Denise said, and his eyes narrowed at her.

"You took long enough to remember that," he said.

"I remembered it."

"At your convenience."

"I told you, that's what matters," she sniffed.

"I suppose you think I ought to be grateful to you for it," Fargo said.

"No need for that. Just be glad your suspicions are backed up by it."

He grunted and lay back on the blanket to gaze out to the lake as the moon trailed its silver reflection across the water. "I still say it's a shame to waste a spot and a night like this," he murmured.

"The world is full of wasted opportunities. Good night." She lay on her back on the blanket, the nightgown falling revealingly against the soft curves of her.

She was right, the world was full of wasted opportunities, Fargo echoed silently as he turned on his side and pulled sleep around him.

3

When morning came he steered a path along the shore of Rainy Lake, headed south, and set a fast pace. The large, irregular-shaped lake began to narrow as the day slid into the afternoon. Fargo finally veered west and they rode up to a high plateau and followed it to where it rolled downward. He drew to a halt at the edge of a line of fragrant-leafed black walnut and motioned to the clear blue body of water ahead of them, rounded at one end with a long, narrow, taillike extension at the other. "Crane Lake," he said, and swept the nearest edge with a long, slow glance. A slope of black walnut and box elder rose to his left, and he gestured for Denise to follow as he sent the Ovaro up through the trees. "Look for a cabin, a shack, anything," he said to her. "We'll stay back and go around the lake."

He rode slowly, paralleling one side of the narrow, taillike portion of the lake. They circled the end and started back along the other side, carefully staying on the tree-covered slope. He had almost reached the spot where the lake began to widen when he spied the cabin, perhaps a dozen yards back from the shore. Denise followed his gaze, nodded, and fell behind him as he moved slowly down the slope. When the cabin came into clear view, he halted and slid from the horse. Denise at his heels, he moved another hundred yards closer on foot and dropped to one knee.

He saw four horses tethered outside the cabin, and as he watched, a man emerged with a bucket and walked to the lake, filled it, and carried it back.

"He's one of Colson's men. He was at the house when I arrived," Denise whispered.

Fargo caught the sound of voices from inside the cabin, leaned against a tree trunk, and settled down to wait. He saw Denise watching intently, her face tight with impatience. As the sun began to slide below the tops of the distant hills, perhaps an hour after they'd begun watching, four men emerged from the cabin and Fargo heard the sharp gasp from Denise.

"There's Colson," she hissed.

Fargo's eyes followed her as she pointed and he saw a well-built man, clothed in a black shirt and black trousers, a man who was younger than he'd expected, with a face most women would call handsome. It was a handsome face, Fargo decided, but one with an edge of ruthlessness behind the good looks, a mouth too tight, dark eyes that were cold and quick as they peered north along the shore of the lake.

"Where the hell are Stevens and the others? They should've been here days ago," Tom Colson muttered, and his cold, quick eyes continued to sweep the lakeshore. "They've had plenty of time to get here."

"Stevens was one of the men you killed back at the house," Denise whispered.

"Figured as much," Fargo said. "And it explains something that's been sticking in the back of my mind." Denise's glance questioned, and he went on, his voice hardly above a whisper. "He wanted you taken. That was the whole idea of you there as a stand-in for Julie Hudson, to buy extra time to get away with her. I kept wondering why his guards put up such a fight for you. But his waiting for them now explains that."

"How?" Denise asked.

"They weren't supposed to put up a real fight. They

were to make it look good but let you be taken," Fargo said.

"Then why'd they put up such a fight for me?"

Fargo's smile was wry. "They saw a Crow Indian making off with you, not who they expected. That threw their whole plan into a cocked hat. They came out fighting and now Colson's still waiting for them."

"And I still don't have the money he owes me," Denise said.

"You've a one-track mind, honey," Fargo murmured, breaking off further talk as Colson barked orders to his men.

"Get some firewood so's we can make coffee," the man snapped as he turned and strode back into the cabin.

Fargo's lips pursed as thoughts leapt inside him and he looked to where the purple-gray of dusk rolled down to blanket the land. He beckoned to Denise to follow as he began to climb back to where they had left the horses.

"What do we do now?" she asked as he halted beside the Ovaro.

"Settle down and wait for morning," Fargo answered.

"Wait for morning?" She frowned in protest. "He's here now, practically in your hands. Why don't you just take him?"

"Four to one, with no good way to surprise them," Fargo said. He led the way to a pair of entwined box elder just out of sight of the cabin. "We can bed down here safely," he said as the dusk turned to dark.

"I don't like waiting. Things always happen you don't expect. He's down there under my nose with my money," Denise protested.

"That's all you care about, isn't it?"

"Never said anything else."

"Guess that's true enough."

"You want Julie Hudson. I want the money Colson owes me."

"Leave it to me and I'll get your money and Julie Hudson," Fargo said. "Now, it's been a hard day's riding. Get yourself some sleep." He took the Ovaro by the cheek strap and started up the hill.

"Where are you going?" Denise asked at once.

"Up a ways. It's best we separate, just in case any of them wander around," he told her.

It was the only answer that came to mind quickly, and he was relieved when she accepted it without protest. "Whatever you say," she muttered, and slid down against the base of a tree trunk.

"Trust me, honey," Fargo said as he moved off, leading the Ovaro. He was quickly swallowed up in the darkness. He climbed a few dozen yards and halted, folded himself down beside a tree, and leaned his head back and closed his eyes. He let himself catnap but made certain not to take more than an hour. He rose again, led the Ovaro downhill, moved slowly, and halted for a moment to peer into the trees where he'd left Denise. He saw her form, her back to him, near the tree, and he made a wide circle as he continued on down the hill.

The cabin came into sight, flickering lamplight streaming out through the open door, and he moved closer to halt where the trees ended. A dozen yards of cleared land separated him from the cabin, and his glance flicked to where the horses were tethered. There were still four, he noted with grim satisfaction. He draped the Ovaro's reins over a low branch, dropped to one knee, and drew the big Colt from its holster as the voices from inside grew louder and he saw the shadows in the doorway. Two men stepped out, then Colson emerged, followed by the fourth man.

"Wait another day. If Stevens and the others don't show up, then you come meet me," Colson said to the others. "If they show up, bring them."

"Yes, sir," one of the others said, a small man with a small mustache on a mousy face.

Colson started to move toward the horses when the voice halted him in his tracks as it came from the darkness. "I want the rest of my money," it said.

"Goddamn," Fargo hissed to himself. "Goddamn her stinking, stubborn hide." Denise's supple, long-waisted figure materialized out of the darkness as she came forward and Fargo saw Tom Colson's eyes widen in astonishment.

"What in hell are you doing here?" Colson asked.

"You know what I'm doing here. I just told you. I want the rest of what you owe me," Denise said.

Colson frowned at her. "How the hell did you find this place?"

"I followed you," Denise said.

"Not alone you didn't, never in a thousand years. You're no damn tracker," Colson said.

"That's right, I didn't do it alone, and that's why you'll do what I say. You're going to give me the rest of the money you promised me and I'll forget the things I know," Denise said.

"And if I don't?" Colson questioned.

"I'll remember everything I heard loud and clear," Denise snapped.

Fargo watched Colson's lips purse as he stared at Denise. "You're a surprise. I really never expected to be seeing you again," the man said.

"Your mistake," Denise bit out.

"Seems so," Colson said. "I guess you win," he added, admission and defeat in his voice, and Fargo groaned inwardly. The rest happened all at once. Denise visibly relaxed at Colson's words when the man lashed out, seized her by the arm, and yanked her forward. He had his other arm around her neck instantly as he pinned her to him. "No, your mistake, honey," Colson said. "This is too important to let a nothing like you get in the way." He flung her at two of the men who caught her and pulled her arms behind her at once. "Take care of her," he ordered.

Fargo, still silently cursing at Denise, raised the Colt as he raised his voice. "Let the girl go," he said, and Colson and the other three men whirled to stare in the direction of his voice. "Let her go," he said again.

While the others stayed frozen, the small man with the small mustache yanked out his six-gun and began firing into the trees. Fargo ducked as the wild shots sprayed around him, fired off a single shot, and the man flew backward, his mustache suddenly stained with splatterings of blood that coughed up from his lips.

Colson and the other two men fell back against the outside wall of the cabin, only inches from the doorway. One of the men pressed the mouth of his six-gun against Denise's cheek. "Shoot and her head comes off," the man snarled. Colson began to move away from the other two men then bolted outright for the horses.

"Take care of it," he yelled back as he leapt onto his horse and started to race away.

Fargo brought the Colt up but the man holding Denise called out.

"You shoot and she gets it, mister," the man called, and Fargo cursed silently as he lowered the gun and Colson disappeared into the night. He stared at Denise as the two men began to edge to the doorway with her, and he cursed her damn, stubborn hide. He felt like leaving her but even as he enjoyed the thought for an instant, he knew he wouldn't.

The hoofbeats of Colson's horse died away and one of the two men called out again, "Drop your gun or she's dead."

"Shoot her and you're both dead. Count on it," Fargo countered. "Let her go and you stay alive."

They reached the doorway and with a quick motion pulled themselves and Denise into the cabin. "Drop the gun, mister. Ten seconds," the one threatened as they disappeared from view. "We'll kill her, sure as hell we will," the man's voice continued. "Ten seconds, nine seconds, eight seconds," he began to count.

Fargo's lips pressed hard. The men were both desperate and scared, at the edge of panic. Colson had raced off and one of them had been blown away before their eyes. They could kill Denise by accident, a nervous pressure on the trigger, anything that could set them off.

"Seven seconds," the one called out. "Six, five, four . . . throw the damn gun in here . . . three, two . . ."

"All right," Fargo called out, and lowered the Colt. He flung it, sent it skittering through the open doorway and into the cabin. He instantly reached down and pulled the slender, double-edged throwing knife from the calf holster around his leg and pushed the knife into his belt inside his shirt.

"Walk in here with your hands up," one of the two called, and Fargo obeyed. He stepped into the doorway and saw one man with his gun trained on him while the other took his gun from against Denise's cheek. The one holding Denise pushed her at the second man, who clamped her arm behind her back at once.

Fargo watched the man come toward him, a narrow, almost sunken face with deep-set eyes, his gun upraised in one hand. There would be a moment when the man would be between himself and the other gunslinger, Fargo knew, a split second when he'd halt to bring the gun down and fire. He waited, watched, counted off seconds as he peered past the advancing man. The sunken-faced man came closer and Fargo's eyes stayed on the figure holding Denise until suddenly the nearest man was directly in front of him. The man halted, blocked out the figure across the room for an instant as he raised his gun.

"So long, mister. We'll take good care of your girlfriend," the man said.

Fargo's hand shot out with the speed of a rattlesnake's strike, his fingers closing around the wrist of the man's gun hand as he forced the man's arm upward. Two shots rang out and slammed into the top of the door frame as the man's fingers automatically tightened on the trigger. But at the same instant, Fargo used his other hand to grab the man's shirt and, using the steel muscles of his legs, flung himself backward out of the doorway, taking the man with him.

As he hit the ground, still holding on to his opponent, Fargo rolled and brought the man beneath him. Retaining his grip on the wrist of the man's gun hand, he drew his right arm back and drove his forearm into the man's throat with all the strength and weight he could bring to bear. He heard the man's gargled, shuddering gasp as the small bones of his larynx collapsed, but Fargo was already rolling, yanking the thin-bladed throwing knife from inside his shirt.

The second man would be racing from the cabin, he knew, and he had all but flattened himself on the ground just as, true to expectations, the figure raced out of the doorway, spraying shots in all directions. The man skidded to a halt outside the doorway, took a moment to stare at the crumpled figure on the ground. By the time he lifted his eyes, the double-edged blade was hurtling through the air. The man tried to duck away and the blade caught him just below his ear. It embedded itself to the hilt and the figure clapped both hands to the sides of his head, executed a strange jog, not unlike a disjointed puppet, before collapsing in a heap.

Fargo pushed to his feet, took three long strides, and retrieved the throwing knife. He wiped it clean on the grass, returned it to the calf holster, and stepped into the cabin. Denise stood against the far wall, her beige eyes wide with fear and uncertainty. When she saw him, the relief pushed the fear from her eyes; she swayed for a moment and caught herself, fighting down the impulse to collapse. She held a poker in one hand, he saw, hard-nosed to the end.

Fargo shook his head in reluctant admiration. "You can put that down," he said, and she let the poker fall from her fingers. He fastened her with a baleful stare. "I ought to tan your damn hide," he growled.

She had the conscience to look apologetic. "I thought I could make him give me my money."

"By holding something over his head? By black-mailing him into it?"

"That's right," she sniffed.

Fargo made a derisive sound. "Chickens don't black-mail hawks," he said. "All you did was nearly get yourself killed and ruin everything for me."

"What were you doing here?"

"I knew Colson was going off tonight. I was going to follow him. He'd have led me right to Julie Hudson."

"How'd you know that?"

"He told the others to get firewood to make coffee. A man staying the night would've told them to get wood to cook supper. He figured only to wait a little longer, get some good riding coffee under his belt, and take off."

"You were going to follow him and leave me." Denise frowned and managed to look hurt.

"I couldn't follow him close enough with you tagging along."

"You could've told me what you planned on doing," she said, and anger rushed into her eyes.

"You'd have screamed and hollered and argued, and you know it. I wasn't about to wrestle with that," he said. Her glowering silence was its own admission. "This is good-bye, Denise, honey," he said.

"No, wait—" she began.

"Wait, hell," he interrupted. "This is the last time you screw up everything by not following orders. I'm tired of your holding out on me, too." He turned and strode from the cabin. She had information he very much wanted, but it'd be a mistake to let her know it. It was time to face her down once and for all. He heard her hurrying after him as he halted beside the Ovaro.

Her hand came out to pull at his arm. "I'm sorry, really I am."

"You've run out of sorry, honey," Fargo said harshly, and prepared to swing onto the horse.

"All right, I promise," Denise said.

He paused, looked hard at her. "Promise what?"

"No more doing anything on my own. No more holding out."

His hard glare stayed. "Talk's cheap," he grunted.

"I know where he's going with Julie Hudson," she said, and Fargo waited grimly. "Colson's taking her to the Mesabi Range."

"The Mesabis? Why?"

"I don't know. I just overheard him say that."

Fargo thought aloud as he frowned into the night. "The Mesabi Range is due south, hard country, mountains, high rock with plenty of deep gorges, iron-ore mines all over it, most emptied out, a few still operating. It'd be good country to hide out if that's what he's planning to do."

"I don't know, but somehow I didn't get that feeling. I never heard any talk of it," Denise said. "What do we do now? Go there?"

"We?"

"I kept part of my promise. I ought to get a chance to keep the rest," she flared.

"All right," he relented. "You've got it."

"So what do we do now?" she asked again.

"We wait till morning and I'll pick up his trail. He's probably going to pick up Julie Hudson someplace before heading for the Mesabi." Denise fell in step

51

beside Fargo as he led the Ovaro uphill and finally halted at the pair of entwined box elder. "Get some sleep," Fargo said as he lay down on the blanket. He pulled off his gun belt and undressed down to his underdrawers, and he saw Denise watching. "Time to get behind the trees and change," he told her.

"Not tonight," she said. She rose and he felt the furrow slide across his brow as he watched her begin to undo the buttons on her shirt. It hung loosely when she finished, though it still covered her breasts. But her fingers were sure and deft as she unlatched the clips at the waist of the skirt, and then, in one quick, wriggling motion, she was naked before him.

Fargo gazed at the beautiful, full curve of her long breasts, each tipped by a brown-pink nipple on a perfect circle of dark pink. Her long-waisted figure flowed into smoothly curved hips, a flat belly gently sliding into a curly, profuse, black nap that pushed upward over her pubic mound. Her legs, long, slender stems of smooth-skinned whiteness, just avoided being on the thin side.

She dropped to her knees beside him. "I promised no more holding out," she said.

"So you did." Fargo nodded and opened his lips to meet her mouth as she leaned forward and wrapped her arms around him. Her kiss was wet and wanting, her lips working at once, her tongue sliding forward and pulling back again. Against his chest, the warm, soft touch of her breasts sent exciting vibrations through him. He closed one hand around her left breast, gently squeezed its softness, and let his thumb move back and forth across the brown-pink nipple.

"Uuuuhh," she groaned, and turned onto her back, her hand moving up and down his smoothly muscled chest. He drew his mouth from hers, brought it down to the firm nipple, and gently sucked. "Ah . . . aaaaah, oh, God," Denise breathed. She pressed her breast upward, pushing it deeper into his mouth as she made soft, satisfied sounds.

Her hands moved from his chest, slid down his abdomen, down farther, and found his hot, burgeoning maleness. Her fingers closed around him. "Oh, oh . . . oh, jeeez," she cried out, holding on to him as her hips lifted, thrust forward.

He lifted and straddled her; his hands pressed down into the soft skin between her hips and her belly, sliding across the curly black nap. Denise shuddered with delight. He pressed one hand down over the bottom tip of the pubic mound and felt the moistness of the curly nap.

"Ooooooh . . . oooh," she groaned. "Yes, I'm wet . . . I want you, oh, God, I want you, want you." Her hand came down to cover his, to press his fingers under the soft tip and into the roscid darkness. Now she uttered a long, almost plaintive cry. He moved deeper, rubbed gently, and Denise's short, gasped sounds grew lower, turned into deep, shuddering moans.

Her long legs fell apart to come together again around his hips. He brought his torso over her as he drew his hand back from her, and she uttered a half-cry of protest that ended abruptly as he rested his eager, pulsating shaft against the moist tunnel.

"Oh, ooooooh, jeeeez," Denise groaned. "Now, now, now, oh, quick, now." He slid smoothly into her and her body began to tremble at once, a wild quivering that shook her every gasped cry. Once again, as he moved smoothly, deliciously inside her, she drew back and forth with him and her cries turned into the deep, rumbling sounds of absolute pleasure.

Her hands, moving up and down his back, pressing into his shoulders, suddenly came up to clasp his face. She held him as she stared up at him, and her eyes seemed opaque, with a strange yellow light deep inside. It was as though she were in another world as she began to quiver and pump upward, her hips lifting with quickening motion. "Ah, ah, ah . . . oh, God, yes, yes, now . . . noooowww," Denise groaned.

Fargo felt her contractions clasp him, a sweet vise of ecstasy. Her low, throbbing moan rose in pitch, became a spiraling scream. Denise's head arched backward as she screamed, the veins in her neck standing out while her entire, long-waisted body quivered, the two longish breasts shaking until, with a tiny half-sob of despair, she sank onto the blanket to lay still, the only sound the harshness of her heavy breathing.

He lay atop her, stayed in her, and moved slowly. "Oh, jeeeez," Denise breathed. "Nice, oh, God, so nice." Her arms, circled around his neck, pulled his face down into her breasts and she held him there until he finally lay beside her and rose up on one elbow to enjoy the loveliness of her. He ran his hand gently across the soft curves and sweet places.

A slow smile touched Denise's full, red lips. "That's called keeping promises," she murmured.

"It was good, whatever you want to call it," Fargo said.

She smiled again, curled herself against him so that one breast rested in the cup of his hand. "I call it a beginning," she murmured before she fell asleep.

4

She was still wrapped around him when morning came and she woke with a satisfied, feline stretch. Mischievously, she rolled across him and let her breasts brush his face before she swung to her feet. She looked unreasonably fresh and lovely.

Fargo had a moment's difficulty in pushing away the thought that flashed through his mind. "Put something on and you can go down to the lake," he told her, and she quickly donned blouse and skirt. He avoided the cabin as he led the way to the lake and watched Denise shed her clothes again and immerse herself in the water. He took off his own clothes and slipped into the lake, washed, and stayed away from her, congratulating himself on his self-discipline.

When he left the water, he dried off with a towel and tossed it to Denise. He watched her supple beauty as she dried herself and dressed. They ate quickly from a clump of blackberry and he swung onto the Ovaro as soon as they were through. Moving to again skirt the cabin, he rode into the woods and swept the ground and the brush with a careful gaze. Finally he pointed to where pieces of low brush were broken off and the ground showed the hoofprints of a single horse and rider.

"Let's go," he said.

Denise fell in close behind as he began to follow the prints with ease. Colson had made no effort to cover his tracks, and it was just past the noon hour when Fargo pulled up and gestured to a spot beside the light-gray bark of a butternut.

"He stopped to sleep here," Fargo said. He dismounted, pressed the flattened grass with one hand. "I'd guess about six hours back. Let's ride."

He swung onto the horse and set a hard pace for the rest of the day. As dusk grew into darkness, he halted where a stream coursed past a bed of fringe moss. "No sense in trying to follow a trail at night. We're close enough. We'll catch up, come morning," Fargo told Denise.

She dismounted and tethered her horse beside the Ovaro. He took some of the dried-beef strips from his saddlebag, and after they finished eating, he spread the blanket on the soft moss. It had been a hard day's riding and he watched her start to undress.

"Tired?" he asked, and she turned a sly smile his way.

"Not that tired," she murmured before she shook off her skirt and petticoat, gave him a moment to shed clothes, and was in his arms at once, her long-waisted warmth pressing against him. Her mouth came down on his, devouringly, and her long, slender legs moved against his. She lifted them to rub into his groin as her tongue glided back and forth in his mouth. He felt himself rising at once, her warm wanting enveloping him.

His lips parted as she pushed upward, offered first one round mound and then the other. He pulled gently on each, and Denise moaned, a low growling sound that rose in pitch as his maleness found her moist warmth. She dug her fingers into his shoulders. "Yes, oh, jeeeez . . . yes, yes," she cried out, and became a willing, pumping, gasping vessel of desire.

Once again, before she climaxed, the strange yellow light filled her eyes and she stared at him as if suddenly in some other world. In a way, she was, he reflected as she began to shake and quiver against him until, head arching backward again, the scream of ecstasy accumulated, desire exploded, spiraling into the darkness. She finally lay under him, her breath a harsh, gasping sound and the very tips of her breasts still quivering.

She stirred at last, and her fingers traced little unseen lines across his chest. "It's not all keeping promises. I wanted you to know that."

"Meaning what?" Fargo questioned.

"Meaning I really like you. You've done things for me you didn't have to, and you're nice to be with," she said.

"I'm flattered."

"Maybe, when this is over, we could stay together?"

"I wouldn't count on that," Fargo said gently but firmly.

"Maybe for a while," she said, an air of plaintiveness in her voice that surprised him.

"Maybe for a while," he allowed.

She pushed up on one arm and her face set. "I'm still going to get the money he owes me. This doesn't change that."

"Didn't think it would." He laughed. "Once a hardnose always a hard-nose." She made a face at him but quickly returned to press herself against his chest and was asleep in minutes. He took a little longer but finally joined her in deep slumber under the soft rustle of the brook.

When morning came, he picked up the trail again. Tom Colson had headed east, not yet on his way to the Mesabi Range, and as Fargo trailed the hoofprints, his eyes swept the terrain. He slowed and pulled into a thicket of black walnut as he spotted a half-dozen near-naked horsemen rounding a turn and moving toward him. They passed far enough away, riding casually, but he managed to discern the markings on the wrist gauntlet worn by one. "Yankton Dakota," he whispered to Denise.

They stayed in the thicket until the red men were completely out of sight. He'd lost at least a half-hour, he estimated, before he picked up the trail again, and he set a faster pace until the hoofprints of Colson's horse turned into a small draw.

He slowed, moved carefully forward, his ears tuned for the slightest sound. He halted at the bottom of the draw and surveyed the scene: the charred-wood remains of a camping fire, the patterns on the ground made by sleeping figures and the hoofprints that covered the area. "They were waiting here for him," Fargo said.

"Who?" Denise asked.

"The rest of his men. Julie Hudson, too, I'd guess," Fargo said, his eyes scanning the ground again. "At least five horses, maybe six. Can't tell for sure." His eyes followed the tracks that went on past the spot. "They left at the other end of the draw." The draw rose in a shallow climb and they halted again when they reached the top. "That way," he muttered. "South, now. I'd say he was heading for the Mesabi Range this time."

The trail was clear and easy to follow and Fargo held to his estimate of five or six horses, riding mostly bunched together. He kept a steady pace that gained ground but the night came all too soon. He pulled into a forest thicket to camp. "They'll bed down, too. We won't be losing time," he said.

"Then let's make the most of it," she said, folding herself into his arms at once. She made the night pass quickly and sleep a welcome intermission.

The morning dawned with a warm sun and Fargo skirted the lakes that dotted the trail until he veered off and took them into the higher hill forests.

"Won't you lose their trail up here?" Denise questioned.

"I've been watching the way they're going. Colson's taking the deer trails and any easy passages. He's not pushing through tree cover or breaking brush. I can pick out where he'll go now without seeing the trail." When the noon hour passed, he halted at a ledge of rock that let him see for miles in any direction.

"How far to the Mesabi?" Denise asked.

"Another three or four days' ride. We'll be catching up to them long before we reach the Mesabi," Fargo told her. His eyes were narrowed as he peered across into the distant low hills. "There's a passel of riders way off in those hills, moving fast," he said. "Been riding in the same direction we are all day."

"I don't see anything," Denise said.

"You can't see them all the time. They're not sending up dust clouds. You watch the movement of the brush and low tree branches," he told her.

"Indians?" Denise asked.

"Maybe. Maybe anything."

"They following us?"

Fargo grunted derisively. "Hell, no. They can't pick us up from there. They're on their own way someplace, I'd guess."

"Same place we are maybe?" Denise suggested.

"Maybe. Maybe not. If so, we'll find out later." Fargo snapped the reins on the Ovaro and moved forward again. He stayed in the trees and the hilly terrain and followed the passages he saw open up below. The long shadows were beginning to slide across the land when the band of riders appeared below and ahead.

"There they are," Denise gasped. "You found them."

"Didn't expect differently," Fargo said, and his eyes sweeping the riders, he saw that he'd been wrong by one. There were seven horses, one carrying a rider with a shock of very curly, very pastel-yellow blond hair. "Julie Hudson," he murmured.

He slowed the Ovaro enough to stay back but keep the band in sight. It wasn't more than another hour, the dusk descending fast, when Colson halted where a pair of tall stones formed the back and sides of a small hollow. Fargo stopped the Ovaro and watched as Julie Hudson dismounted along with the others. Distance prevented a really good view of her but he saw an even-featured face with round cheeks under the very pale blond hair. Her compact figure was attired in dark-blue riding britches and a light-blue shirt.

He watched as the group began to set up camp for the night and the girl helped tether the horses to one side. "No ropes on her. Nobody watching her. She's no prisoner," Fargo commented.

"Did you think she was?" Denise frowned.

"I thought she might be, especially from the way Cyrus Reiber talked that Colson was making off with her," Fargo said. "But she's sure as hell not." As he watched, some of the men made a small fire and the camp was set up against the two rock walls. Julie Hudson sat down beside Colson, Fargo saw. But a grim smile touched his face as Colson set out two sentries to cover the front of the camp with the stone walls securing the back and sides. "Shit," he muttered, drawing a stare from Denise. "I figured to take her later in the night, but it'll be damn near impossible the way that spot sets up. I don't want to go in shooting. She could get a stray bullet."

"That the only reason?" Denise asked, and Fargo tossed her a wry smile. Her instincts were working overtime.

"No," he admitted. "There's too much I don't know about this whole thing."

"You still going to take her?" Denise asked.

"Yes, but I'll wait. Maybe they'll set down in a

better spot tomorrow." He turned the Ovaro deeper into the hills, found a quiet place, swung to the ground, and prepared to bed down.

Denise came to him and made love with a tenderness under her passion and the night slowly passed into a warm morning.

He woke first, used his canteen to wash, and quickly dressed. He went down the hill to where he could watch the camp below, and saw them preparing to move. Below, Julie Hudson, her pale-blond hair glistening in the new sun, rode from the camp beside Tom Colson and the other five followed close behind.

Denise joined Fargo, leading the horses, and he took to the saddle at once. Again, he stayed back, content to just keep the riders below in sight.

Colson set a leisurely pace, halting at a stream when the noon sun hung high. When he rode on, Julie Hudson was at his side again. Fargo's eyes swept the terrain on all sides as he rode, and when Colson halted once more, the trailsman's glance lingered on the distant hills.

"Those other riders still there?" Denise asked.

"Still there, still riding their own course," Fargo said.

When Colson rode on again, Fargo sent the Ovaro forward and saw the riders below start to go into rolling-hill country, heavily foliaged on all sides. Colson still followed the easy path of deer trails and rainwashed passages; the man rode with casual ease. Colson hardly glanced at the hills or at the thick forest land that surrounded him. He was either stupid or completely unaware of the terrain he traveled, Fargo decided. He felt his own lips tighten as, a half-hour further on, he reined to a halt abruptly.

"What is it?" Denise asked quickly, and Fargo pointed to the line of unshod pony prints.

"Indian ponies," he said.

"The ones we saw yesterday?"

"No, these are fresh, not over an hour old and coming from the southwest. I count twelve horses," Fargo said. He sent the Ovaro forward, but now his gaze all but ignored the riders below as his eyes probed the hills. He had ridden for a little more than an hour when he reined up again, this time nodding to the line of shagbark hickory a few dozen yards ahead.

Denise followed his gesture and her eyes widened as she saw the line of twelve horsemen, hardly visible in the trees, as they peered down at Colson and the others riding below. Fargo took in the markings on the browband of the nearest figure as all sat silent as stone carvings. "Yankton Dakota," he muttered to Denise. Some were carrying carbines, some lances, and others bow and arrows.

In the center of the row, a brave with a slender but hard-muscled body raised his arm halfway into the air, a carbine in his hand.

"They're going to attack," Denise whispered.

"And Colson's going to be taken completely offguard. He's not alert to a damn thing," Fargo said grimly, and glanced at the frown Denise pushed his way. "Don't say it," he growled.

"I certainly am going to say it. If you warn them, they can take cover and beat off the attack," she snapped.

"And if I race down to warn them, they'll know I'm here, following. After they fight off the Dakota, they'll stay on guard from here on. I'll never get Julie Hudson if I can't surprise them."

"If you don't warn them, all you'll have is a dead Julie Hudson," Denise muttered.

Fargo cursed at the truth in her words. It was no damn good either way, but his brow took on a deep furrow of thought as he peered at the Dakota. "There might be one way," he said, thinking aloud as he lifted his eyes to sweep the hills, seeking out each path and gully. "If I can get the Dakota to chase me, they'll be warned below but all they'll see is a glimpse of the Dakota chasing after somebody."

"But you can't let them come after you. That'd be suicide. They'll catch you for sure," Denise said.

"Not for sure—not if I do it right," Fargo said not without a grimness in his voice. "Get off your horse and lie down deep in the high brush over there. You stay there, no matter what you hear. They'll be charging past you real close, but you stay down. Promise?"

"Promise." Denise nodded, apprehension in her face.

"You stay down till I get back or it gets dark," he said.

"I don't like the sound of that."

"But you'll do it whether you like it or not," Fargo insisted, and she nodded unhappily. "Now," he hissed, and watched Denise disappear into the thick, high brush. He looked back at the line of braves and drew the Sharps from its saddle case. The one in the center was starting to raise his arm higher as Colson passed below.

Fargo took quick aim, fired, and saw the Indian bend to one side and clutch at his shoulder as the carbine fell from his hand. The others turned as one, but Fargo was already racing through the trees, pulling Denise's horse along with him. He stayed in the thick tree cover, though it slowed him, and he heard the wild whooping shouts of the Yankton Dakota as they started in pursuit.

Below, Colson and the others had heard the shot and were already taking cover, he knew. They'd be peering up into the hills and see flashes of the Indians streaking through the trees.

Fargo turned the Ovaro toward a narrow path he had already noted. Just before he reached it, he slapped Denise's horse on the rump and sent the animal racing on uphill. He rode hard into the small path lined on both sides with the slender branches of young shingle oak, and heard some of his pursuers chase after Denise's horse while others followed into the narrow path after him. He took the Ovaro almost to the end of the path before he leapt from the saddle and sent the horse racing on. He landed with both feet and dived into the low brush behind the trees, the big Sharps in hand.

Silence was all-important to his plan. He crouched and listened to the Dakota coming fast. He yanked the narrow, double-edged throwing knife from its calf holster and transferred the rifle to his left hand. The Dakota came down the pathway, riding hard, four of them, he counted, one carrying a lance, the other three bows and arrows. He stayed crouched low until the first three passed, and when the fourth rode by, a few yards back of the others, he flung the knife with all his strength and accuracy. The blade hurtled through the air with silent deadliness, struck the Indian between the shoulder blades, and embedded itself to the hilt. The Dakota flung both arms outward as he toppled from the side of his horse, hit the ground, and lay still.

Fargo ran from the brush, retrieved the throwing knife, wiped it clean on the grass, and dragged the Indian into the brush. He picked up the man's bow and his elkskin quiver of arrows and retreated into the low brush to wait.

It was not a long wait and he had an arrow resting on the bowstring as the first of the other three came back down the path. The Indian rode slowly, carefully, bow and arrow in one hand ready to fire. His black eyes searched the path, and a frown creased his red-skinned brow. Fargo, the bow already drawn, let the arrow fly in a short, straight trajectory and saw the flint-pointed arrowhead shatter the Indian's breastbone. The Dakota shuddered, his mouth dropping open as he fell silently forward against the neck of his pony, hung there for a moment, and fell to the ground.

Fargo had another arrow on the drawn bowstring as the third brave appeared. The Indian pulled to a halt as he saw the crumpled figure on the ground. He raised his eyes just in time to see the arrow hurtling at him and he tried to twist aside, but the shaft pierced his naked abdomen, hung there quivering as a small shower of red began to turn it scarlet.

As the Dakota fell to the ground, the trailsman dropped the bow and quiver, picked up the big Sharps, and ran past the slain men. He kept running to where the path ended, then he veered to one side and ducked behind a tree as the remaining brave of the four following him appeared, entered the path, and began to ride back down its narrow passage.

Fargo spied the Ovaro, halted in the trees, and ran on silent steps to the horse. He stayed on foot but pulled the horse into the thick tree cover and listened to the sound of the other Dakota moving back and forth through the hillside. They were making uncertain, tentative probes. He moved forward as he saw one horseman riding toward him. He took his lariat from the saddle, left the Ovaro hidden amid the trees, and crept forward.

Fargo wanted one more dead and unfound, and he watched that one come into clear view. The brave carried a carbine, Fargo noted as he let the Indian pass and began to follow the slow-moving horse. The brave kept the slow pace, searching into the trees with every step, and Fargo silently followed. When the Dakota came to a spot where the trees thinned, Fargo stepped out into the clear and sent the lariat spinning through the air. The rope came down over the startled Indian's head and Fargo yanked the loop tight around his neck. The man flew backward over the horse's rump as Fargo yanked, and hit the ground hard on the back of his neck. Fargo heard the sharp sound of vertebrae cracking and the figure twitched and lay still.

The shout came from below, along the path, and Fargo quickly pulled the Indian into the brush and trees and removed the lariat. The two slain braves on the path had been discovered.

Fargo listened to the sound of ponies hurrying down to the path. They would gather in a strained and uneasy conference, he knew, and it was exactly what he counted on happening. Their leader wounded, two of their warriors found slain and two missing, and none of those remaining had glimpsed the enemy. It would not sit well at all. The Indian was a fierce fighter of unquestioned bravery in the field. But he disliked fighting the unknown. Beliefs were never far from behavior, and the Indian believed in omens, good and bad. An unseen wraith of a foe who had slain four of their number and wounded their leader could well be a bad omen, a sign to flee. That's what they'd do, he felt certain, and he stayed in the trees, his ears tuned to the first sound from below.

It came soon enough, horses moving upward at a steady pace. In the distance through the heavy forest foliage, he glimpsed the file of horsemen moving up the hill. He let a long sigh of relief escape his lips. It had worked: they were leaving. He rose to his feet but stayed in the thick tree cover. When the last sound died away, he moved forward, leading the Ovaro behind him, and he paused again, sank to one knee, and listened. But there was no sound to send him racing. The Dakota had continued on their way.

He rose, swung onto the Ovaro, and sent the horse along the side of the hill above the beginning of the narrow pathway. He scanned the woods and finally spied the brown form standing quietly beneath the branches of a black walnut. He collected Denise's horse and made his way down the hill to where he had left her.

He halted, finally, slipped to the ground, and stared into the high brush. "You can come out, honey," he said. A moment of silence followed and then her head pushed upward, beige eyes wide, the fine, gossamer brown hair flecked with bits and pieces of leaf and brush.

"Oh, God. Oh, good God," Denise breathed. She burst from the brush to fall into his arms. "You have no idea what it was like, hearing so many sounds and having to just lay there."

"It wasn't exactly a picnic outside, either," Fargo said laconically, and she drew back and kissed him.

"No, of course not," she murmured. "But you're here. That's all that counts."

"For now."

She clung a moment longer and then stepped back. "What now?"

"We go back to watching Colson," Fargo said. They immediately started down the hill, continuing until he reached a spot that afforded a good view of the passage below. He sank down on one knee with Denise and settled down to wait.

It was perhaps a half-hour later when he saw Colson and one of his men cautiously step from the trees where they'd taken cover, their eyes sweeping the hills. Another man came forward, then another, and the last to show was Julie Hudson. All scanned the hills, grim apprehension on each face. Then, finally convinced the Indians had left, they brought their horses out, mounted, and started on their way. But now Colson and the others rode with their eyes constantly flicking to the forests and hills that surrounded them.

Fargo waited till they were a good distance ahead

before following again, keeping inside the heavy tree cover of the hills. "There's only about an hour of daylight left," he said, noting the long shadows already sliding down the hills. "They'll have to find a place to bed down soon."

As the shadows continued to grow longer, Fargo followed the riders below and he spotted the small lake before they did. When Colson reached it in the early dusk, he quickly settled down to camp at the edge of the water.

"He figures to use the lake at his back. That way he'll only have to have sentries face out in one direction," Fargo said, and a grim smile crossed his face. The smile stayed as he saw the horses being tethered together at one side of the area. He nudged Denise. "You see Julie Hudson's horse, second from the left end?" he asked, and she nodded. "Mark it in your mind," he said.

"Why?" She frowned.

"We can't get away unless she has a horse to ride," Fargo said. "While I get her, you'll get her horse."

"Now, just hold on. I've never done anything like this before!"

"I'm sure you've said that about a lot of things at one time or another."

"Very funny."

"I'll spell it all out for you. All you have to do is do it," he said, and tossed her a smile of confidence. He sat down against a box elder and watched the campsite below in the last of the dusk. He saw Julie Hudson take her blanket and set it out not far from the water's edge, and he nodded in satisfaction. Before night fell, he watched Colson set out two sentries at the perimeter of the camp where it faced the forested hills, and as night descended, Fargo took some hardtack from his saddlebag and silently ate with Denise facing him.

He waited, letting the moon rise to bring its ghostly

patina to the land before he began to talk to Denise. He laid out his plan for her and took it step by step, detailing what he had mapped out for himself and what he had delegated to her. She listened, her face grim as he went over each step again, including alternate moves if needed. "It has to go off like clockwork to succeed," he told her when he finished.

"What if something goes wrong or I make a mistake?"

"Things can always go wrong. That's not the same as making a mistake. You don't make mistakes," he said harshly.

She let her cheeks puff out as a long sigh escaped her. "Yes, sir," she said with a touch of tartness.

The Trailsman leaned back and waited until the camp below was at peace before he rose and glanced down at the campsite. He could just make out the two guards and the other prone, still shapes on the ground.

He began to undress until he was stripped almost naked. He put his gun belt back on again and tossed a smile at Denise.

"See you soon," he said, and she nodded unhappily, watching as he disappeared into the night. He moved in a straight line through the trees until he was past sight of the camp. He turned left and began to climb down the forest-covered hillside till he reached the shore of the lake some hundred yards beyond where Colson and the others were encamped. He slipped into the warm water as noiselessly as a cottonmouth and began to paddle toward the camp. As he drew closer, he sank beneath the surface, and when he came up, he was opposite the campsite. He let himself tread water while he peered at the shoreline in front of him and noted the two guards at the far edge of the camp, their backs to him. Everyone else lay asleep and he quickly picked out Julie Hudson, pale hair a silvery yellow under the moonlight.

She was closer to the water's edge than it had appeared from above, and he uttered a silent grunt of satisfaction. He stayed in place, continuing to tread water as he gave Denise time to take up her position. Finally, he stopped treading water and let the current push him to shore. He crawled from the lake on his belly, pausing to peer across the sleeping campsite at the guards. Their backs stayed toward him and he inched forward again, crawling toward Julie Hudson's sleeping form. He halted, dropped his cheek down to the grass as one of the guards half-turned and glanced back across the camp. When the man returned to peering into the dark hills, Fargo crawled forward again and felt the tiny beads of perspiration that had come to his face.

He drew close enough to Julie Hudson to see she wore blue cotton pajamas. He halted within inches of her and his lips tightened. This was the dangerous and delicate moment. Silence was imperative. He had to quickly apply enough pressure on her to put her out, but too much would put her out permanently. He reached out, his one hand clamping over her mouth, and he saw blue eyes snap open instantly. But his other hand was against her neck, pressing just below one ear, and he watched her eyes widen, turn dull, and close; her body went limp. He rose up on one knee, scanned the camp and the guards again: their backs were still toward him. He lifted Julie Hudson, strode the few feet to the water, and dropped to the ground with her.

Sliding into the water, he pulled her in after him, held her limp, unconscious form close to him as he kept her head above the water. Holding her with one arm wrapped around her neck, he drew the Colt, lifted it high, and fired two shots. He saw the guards spin and start running toward the water. The signal to Denise had exploded in the night, and as he watched, he saw the two guards skid to a halt on their way to the shore and spin to peer toward where the horses were tethered. The sound of racing hoofbeats came to his ears and he saw the rest of the camp come awake. He struck out with Julie Hudson's unconscious figure, one arm around her neck, and he glimpsed those in the camp running toward where the horses had been, but they had by now galloped away. Some of the men turned back to stare into the lake, but Fargo was in the darkness now, swimming toward the shore some fifty yards down from the camp.

When he reached the shore, he rose, tossed Julie Hudson over his shoulder, and began to climb up the hillside until he saw the place where he'd left Denise. She was there, holding Julie's horse. He grinned approvingly at her as he put Julie on the ground. "Good. I knew you could do it," he said.

"I'm glad you knew it," she returned. "They were all confused, just as you said they'd be. They ran to the lake first, then back the other way when they heard the horses running."

Fargo bent over Julie Hudson and saw she was still unconscious. He picked her up and draped her across the saddle of her horse on her stomach. "They won't round their horses up till daylight. Let's make a little more time meanwhile," he said, and dried himself with a towel, dressed, and climbed onto the Ovaro. He led the way across the hills and halted after a little over an hour as Julie Hudson began to make small sounds of waking. "We'll bed down here," he said.

Denise dismounted as he lifted Julie Hudson to the ground. She blinked at him and he saw large, round blue eyes, a round-cheeked face, softly pretty, with a Cupid's-bow mouth of full lips, almost a doll-like, little-girl face. The loose pajamas pretty much hid the rest of her, and he stepped back as she blinked again and her round eyes peered at him.

"Who are you?" she asked, a soft, tinkly voice.

"We'll talk in the morning," he said. "Right now I want to get some sleep. I'm going to tie you up, honey, till we can talk more." He took a length of lariat and quickly tied her wrists and ankles and set her down against a tree.

"This isn't necessary," she said without anger.

"I apologize, but it's staying," Fargo said. He walked from her to a tree, set out his blanket, and Denise lay down beside him. He was aware of Julie Hudson watching him with quiet curiosity as he fell asleep.

When the morning sun woke him with its warming rays, he sat up and his eyes went to Julie Hudson at once. She was awake, watching as he rose and pulled Denise to her feet, and he went to her and untied her bonds. "Take your things and get dressed," he said, and she nodded, her round blue eyes showing more curiosity than anything else. He watched her take her canteen and a clothes bag from her horse and go into the trees to finally reappear in the dark-blue riding britches and a white shirt. Fargo took in a very curvaceous figure, compact and filling the britches with a round rear. Her small waist blossomed upward to high, very round breasts that pushed the white shirt out deliciously.

"You're the one, aren't you?" she asked in her tinkly voice, and he again had the impression of a little girl inside a very womanly body.

"The one?" Fargo echoed.

"Tom said we were being followed," Julie explained. "But he said you were the scout for bandits and thieves."

"He lied," Fargo said simply.

Julie turned her eyes to Denise. "I didn't expect you'd have a companion," she said, and again he heard only a curiousness in her voice.

"I've my own business with Tom Colson," Denise snapped.

72

"I'm afraid I'm quite confused," Julie replied, and her round blue eyes blinked at Fargo. Her pale-yellow hair topping the round-cheeked face gave her a doll-like quality and a kind of sweetness, he decided.

"I'm Fargo, Skye Fargo, and this is Denise Farr," he said.

"Hello, Denise," Julie said with a warm smile that Denise answered with a wary frown.

"We've some talking to do," Fargo said. "But I'm no scout for a bunch of sidewinders."

Julie Hudson's blue eyes peered at him. "If you say so," she answered.

"You just going to believe him?" Denise cut in, frowning at the other woman.

"Yes," Julie Hudson said. "I don't have a problem believing people. I think we don't believe each other enough. Most times people are honest."

"Hah!" Denise snorted. "Where the hell have you been living, honey?"

Fargo watched Julie turn to Denise, a soft chiding in her voice as she replied, "We all make the worlds we live in."

Denise's lips tightened.

"We'll talk more later. Right now we ride," Fargo said.

"Whatever you say." Julie walked to her horse. She put her things on the saddlehorn and swung into the saddle with her round, high breasts pressing the shirt into smooth mounds.

"Jesus," Denise muttered to Fargo.

"She's not what I expected," Fargo allowed.

"She's not for real," Denise snapped.

"She's different than the women you've known. That doesn't make her not real." Fargo smiled understandingly.

Denise shot him a disdainful glance. "She's not for real!"

"Hit the saddle," Fargo said, and smiled inwardly. Denise would have trouble accepting anyone who refuted her own hard-nosed view of life. Absorbing a different set of beliefs might be good for her, he reflected as he climbed onto the Ovaro and sent the horse into a fast trot.

Putting some distance between himself and Colson was first. Finding out more about Julie Hudson would wait.

5

Fargo set a brisk pace southward and followed the hills down to rolling land dotted with lakes and open places along with thick forest. It was afternoon when he drew to a halt beside a narrow river and watered the horses. Denise had ridden in sullen silence, Julie Hudson with cool aplomb, and after both young women refreshed themselves with the water, he watched Julie perch herself upon a rock while Denise leaned back against a tree.

"Let's talk some," Fargo said, and Julie turned her blue eyes on him. She leaned her head back as she gazed speculatively at him, the yellow-blond hair falling in a shimmering cascade that made her look half-little-girl and half-siren.

"You said you're not the scout for a pack of bandits. Then why have you taken me captive?" she asked with firmness.

"Your Uncle Cyrus hired me to take you from Tom Colson," Fargo said, and saw her blond eyebrows lift in surprise and then a sad little smile touch her round-cheeked, sweet face.

"Oh, dear," Julie Hudson murmured. "I'm so sorry Uncle Cy felt he had to do that. But then he's always disliked Tom so much. He never accepted the fact that Tom was a lot younger than Mother and he's always felt Tom used her and is now using me."

"You saying he's wrong about that?" Fargo frowned.

Her sad smile stayed. "I know he has his reasons to feel that way. I can understand them without accepting them."

"You think Tom Colson has your best interests at heart?" Fargo questioned.

"I think so. I think Uncle Cyrus does, too. Neither of them is completely unselfish, but I think they both care about me. That's what makes all this so unnecessary," Julie said, and the sadness was in her voice again. "I told that to Tom, but he wouldn't listen. He just wants to help me."

"He hired Denise to stand in for you and had men waiting to kill me if they could," Fargo said.

"And he stuck me for half the money he promised," Denise cut in. "That doesn't sound like Mr. Nice to me."

Julie frowned thoughtfully for a moment. "No, it doesn't," she agreed. "And maybe he's handled everything badly, but I still think he's trying to do the right thing for me. So is Uncle Cyrus, in his way."

"Jesus, everybody is so damn good-hearted," Denise snorted.

Again, Julie Hudson's reply carried a quiet reprimand: "I think people are, if you give them a chance."

"And they'll screw you if you give them a chance," Denise tossed back.

"Just what is it you think they're trying to do for you?" Fargo questioned Julie. "Colson takes off with you and sets up a fancy scheme to throw everybody off, including hired gunhands. Your uncle hires me to bring you to him and he doesn't care how I do it. Why? What the hell is it all about?"

"I'll tell you. You deserve to know," Julie said, and her smile was apologetic. "When I was a little girl, my real father took me into the Mesabi Range and showed me where he'd hidden a will and a map that told of a fortune in silver he had hidden away. He was sick then

76

and knew he hadn't long to live, though he didn't tell me that. But he said that he was going away, and that if he told anyone else about the fortune in silver, it'd be taken away from me. I was too young to stop that, he said, and he was probably right."

"Probably," Fargo agreed.

"The will was made out so's the fortune would be mine when I turned nineteen, but he wanted to show me where it was hidden, along with the map, so I could get it when the time came."

"Who knew about this will and the map besides you?" Fargo asked.

"I'm sure he told my mother and she probably told Tom after they were married. Then Uncle Cyrus knew. I don't think anybody else," Julie said.

"Why didn't he just leave the will and the map with your mother?" Fargo pressed.

"For the same reasons he didn't give me the silver. He was afraid somebody would take it from her over the years," Julie said.

"Somebody such as Tom Colson?" Denise snapped.

Julie shrugged. "Somebody," she said. "But Daddy made one mistake: he took a little girl, seven or eight years old, into a strange, wild place and expected she'd be able to remember all that he told her."

"And you can't," Fargo said.

"Exactly," she said. "When I turned nineteen, I tried to remember things and realized I couldn't. Mother died and it made remembering even harder. That's when I suggested to Tom that maybe I should go back to the Mesabi Range and see if being there would stimulate my memory. I think it might well, seeing things, moving through places my father led me, being there again. It could jog the memory."

"It could. Familiar things can do that," Fargo agreed.

"I knew I could never go there alone. Goodness knows what might happen to me alone, so Tom agreed to take me," Julie went on. "Of course, I didn't know Uncle Cyrus was so upset about it that he'd hire some-one to take me from Tom."

"Tom Colson knew it and tried to make damn sure that wouldn't happen," Fargo said, and he paused at the next thought that came to his lips. He peered at Julie's round-cheeked, almost naïve sweetness and felt Scrooge-like at his own thoughts. "You ever think that maybe Tom Colson might be doing all this so he can take the silver for himself once you find the map and the will?"

"No, I haven't thought about that, and I don't be-lieve he would," Julie said.

"Maybe you better start thinking about it," Denise interjected. "And the same for good old Uncle Cyrus. That's why they're both so interested in getting you away from the other, I'd say."

"Do you always have such a terrible view of people? I feel sorry for you if you do," Julie asked her.

"It's called being realistic, honey," Denise snapped.

"It's having no faith in the good side of anyone," Julie said.

"Faith is one thing. Being dumb's another," Denise retorted.

Julie just smiled and gave a little shrug. She slipped from the rock to the ground and again Fargo noted how the high, very round breasts tightened inside the white shirt. "No matter," she said, her round eyes on him. "Now that you know everything, you can take me back to Tom," she said.

"Sorry," Fargo said. "I've a deal to deliver you to Cyrus Reiber, and that's what I'm going to do. You settle all the rest of this among yourselves."

"Are you saying you don't believe what I've just told you?" Julie asked. There was real hurt in her voice as her round eyes waited almost with innocence.

"No, I'm not saying that. Fact is, I do believe you," he said.

"I'm glad," Julie said with a warm smile.

"But you could be too trusting. Besides, what I think doesn't matter. I made a deal with Cyrus Reiber and I'll stick by it," Fargo said.

"That's honorable, and I understand," Julie said. "I won't be a problem, no trying to run off. I promise."

"That'll make it a lot pleasanter for everybody." Fargo smiled. "Now let's ride." He climbed onto the Ovaro and put the horse into a slow trot. He headed into high land again. Colson would be chasing after him and he'd make a wide circle before turning back.

Denise came up to ride alongside him while Julie rode a half-dozen yards back. "Why bother taking her back to Reiber?" Denise said. "He lied to you from the start. He never said a damn word about any hidden silver or a map and a will. He just wanted her back to protect her from big bad stepfather."

"I know, and I'm not happy about that," Fargo said. "I'm going to have a little talk with him before I turn Julie over."

"Why?" Denise frowned.

"I don't want to turn her from the frying pan into the fire," Fargo said.

"I'll be damned," Denise said, and he met her stare. "Little Miss Goodness has you protecting her, too."

"It's not a matter of protecting her," Fargo returned even as he realized she was not entirely wrong. "It's a matter of being fair."

"Hah," Denise snorted.

"What would you have me do?" he pushed at her with irritation.

"Go to Colson. Tell him to give me the rest of my money and he gets her back," Denise said instantly. "It'll be fine with her. She believes in him, she says."

"And if she's wrong about that?" he pressed.

"That's not my problem, and since when did it become yours?" Denise glowered.

"Thinking I might have tossed a trusting person to the wolves will stick in my craw," Fargo said. "I like to look at myself every morning and feel right about it."

"You know what?" Denise pushed back. "I don't think she's all that trusting."

"Just what are you saying?"

"I don't know exactly, but I can't swallow all that wide-eyed bullshit," Denise snapped.

"I think you envy her," Fargo remarked. "I think you envy that quality about her."

"Go to hell," Denise shot back, and spurred her horse on.

Fargo laughed, cast a glance back at Julie, and saw her hurry to catch up as he raced on. He passed Denise's angry face and rode on higher into the hills as his eyes searched the terrain. He finally halted at a spot where the hillside leveled off and the trees thinned to let him see down into the low land in all directions. He pointed to the distant cluster of horsemen as Denise pulled up and Julie followed.

"They're still with us," Fargo muttered, his eyes narrowed. Five or six riders, he counted silently, still too far away to make out clearly. But they were riding diagonally toward where he watched from the high land. "You two take a rest here. They're riding this way now. It's time for a closer look," he said, and turned the pinto downhill.

He rode through the trees, not hurrying, took an angle that would bring him into the low ground as the others reached it. He rode unhurriedly, timing his pace with an occasional glimpse of the approaching riders, and he was waiting between two bitternut tree trunks near a stream as the riders came into close view.

He felt a stab of surprise that pushed at him as he saw the horseman in the lead, a bulbous-nosed, red-veined face with his hat pushed back on a head of thinning hair. "I'll be damned," Fargo muttered aloud. He watched the riders come to a halt at the stream, as he expected they might. He glanced at the other five men, all with worn riding gear and equally worn faces, a pickup crew willing to do whatever was asked of them, he was certain. He waited till they were all dismounted and at the stream before he swung from the Ovaro and walked forward. "Surprise, surprise," he said, and saw six heads spin his way with Cyrus Reiber's watery eyes opening wider than the others.

"Fargo," the man muttered, and pushed to his feet.

"In person," Fargo said.

"What are you doing here?" The man frowned.

"That's my question, Cyrus. What are *you* doing here?"

The older man's eyes grew a fraction narrower. "When I didn't hear anything from you, I decided to collect a few boys and come out to look for myself."

"No patience or no confidence?" Fargo asked mildly.

"Taking no chances," the older man bristled. "Maybe something went wrong on your end. I'd no way of knowing," he grumbled.

"Only you haven't been looking around. You've been riding hard for days," Fargo said. "You wouldn't be on your way to the Mesabi Range, would you, Cyrus?" He smiled as Cyrus Reiber's jaw dropped.

"Now, why would I be going there?" Reiber said with an attempt at recovery.

"To try to meet up with Colson and Julie," Fargo said. "You lied to me, Cyrus. You never told me anything about the map and the will and the fortune in silver for Julie."

"Where'd you hear about that?" Reiber frowned.

"Julie told me," Fargo said.

Reiber exploded with instant excitement. "Julie? You've got her?" Greedy anticipation flooded Reiber's red-veined face.

"For now," Fargo said. "I don't like being given half a story, Cyrus."

"I figured it best that way," Reiber answered, and his eyes grew crafty.

"Because you figured I'd decide maybe you want Julie for your good more than for hers?" Fargo pressed.

"No, I didn't figure that, and anyway it's none of your damn business. You've got Julie, then you bring her to me," Reiber demanded.

"I've got to think some more on that," Fargo said calmly.

"Dammit, we made a deal, Fargo," Reiber said.

"You broke it by not leveling with me," Fargo said. He started to turn away.

"I want that girl here. I know what's best for her," Reiber called, but Fargo continued walking toward the Ovaro. "You take another step and I'll have Pete here put a bullet through you, Fargo," Reiber called.

Fargo turned and looked at the man beside Cyrus Reiber, and he smiled slowly. "Don't get Pete killed, Cyrus," he said with quiet advice in his tone. He turned and started toward the horse again.

"Stop him," he heard Reiber bark.

The Trailsman whirled, the big Colt in his hand, and fired before he'd finished the spin. The man beside Reiber had just cleared the holster with his six-gun when the bullet struck. He flew backward as though kicked by a stallion when the heavy bullet slammed into him at close range. He landed with his head in the stream and his abdomen flowing a slow stain of red.

Fargo backed toward the Ovaro but saw the others stayed frozen in fear. He swung onto the horse with a last glance at Cyrus. "I'll be talking to Julie," he told the man, and sent the Ovaro into the trees at a fast canter.

"After him," he heard Reiber shout.

Fargo fully expected the men would do so, and he sent the pinto flashing down a passage, veered and climbed sharply, turned in another sharp maneuver, and sent the horse streaking along a stretch of flatland. They'd have to go slow to follow and not miss a turn, he knew, but they'd keep coming and he wanted to put distance between himself and his pursuers. He doubled back to where Denise and Julie waited and skidded to a halt.

"Hit the saddle," he said, and both young women scrambled onto their horses. He led the way downhill to where he had spotted a narrow river that ran south. He sent the Ovaro into the river, found it shallow, their horses' hooves touching bottom, and he rode through the river, Denise behind him, Julie on her heels. He followed the watery avenue for at least an hour and left it only when it curved west.

The dusk had begun to descend when he found a half-moon-shaped clearing and drew to a halt. "We've enough distance to make a fire to warm the beef jerky," he said. "We won't have to go back to Cy Reiber, either. That was him back there."

Both Denise and Julie shot surprised glances at him. "That was Uncle Cy?" Julie frowned.

"On his way to try to meet you at the Mesabi." Fargo nodded. "Only tomorrow he'll be trying to catch us. So will Colson." He picked up enough small twigs to make a modest fire as the night fell, and warmed the strips of beef jerky.

"I thought you were going to turn me over to Uncle Cyrus," Julie said.

"Haven't said I wouldn't," Fargo answered between bites. "But I want to think some more on it. I'm not sure you ought to be with either of them."

"That's very nice of you to say, Fargo." Julie smiled. "Unexpected compliments are always the nicest."

"I'm going to bed," Denise cut in. She flounced to her feet and took her blanket to the far side of the camp. Julie watched her as she undressed with no attempt at modesty and pulled the nightgown on.

Julie smiled at Fargo. "She has her own ways of being disdainful," she commented.

"She has her own ways for everything," Fargo grunted.

"No matter. I'm tired, too. I'll be turning in," Julie said.

"You bed down on the other side. I'll sleep in the trees, just in case," Fargo said.

Julie nodded obediently, stepped into the brush to change, and returned in the loose pajamas. She seemed even more like a little girl lost in the folds of the pajamas, her round-cheeked face and Cupid's-bow mouth adding to the image. But as she walked toward him, the high, round breasts were anything but little-girlish as they swayed against the top of the pajamas. She followed him into the trees as he pulled his blanket with him, and waited for him to set it down.

"I want to thank you for caring, Fargo," she said, and her hand came up to rest against his chest. "More people should be caring." Her round blue eyes peered up at him, pale-yellow hair falling loosely around her face. "I'll be thinking tomorrow, also," she said seriously.

"Good," he said, and she rose up on the tips of her toes to brush his cheek with her lips, the touch soft as a butterfly's wing. She hurried away at once and he stretched out on the blanket.

Julie Hudson was two people in one, emotionally and physically, he reflected. Emotionally she was naïve and trusting while holding a firm faith in people. Physically she was compact, excitingly so, with a throbbing sexuality and a little-girl sweetness that didn't match the rest of her. A unique little package, he decided, and he closed his eyes to let sleep wrap its blanket around him.

He was awake first when morning came, and he surveyed the land below from a small rock outcrop.

Denise came up to him after she woke and dressed, her face grave. "You're making a mistake," she said coldly.

"About what?"

"About getting involved with little Miss Goodness's problems," she snapped.

"What makes you think I'm going to do that?" Fargo smiled.

"Signs. I know how to read them, too. My kind of signs," Denise answered. "She's not for real. Just remember I told you."

"I'll do that," Fargo said with some annoyance. "And you could try understanding her."

"I am trying, believe me," Denise snorted. She turned away as Julie came up.

"Good morning," Julie sang out cheerily. "I slept well. I hope everyone else did."

"The pure in heart always sleep well," Denise said, sarcasm draped over each word. Julie only smiled back.

"Mount up. We'll be riding out right away," Fargo ordered. He watched both young women gather their gear, Denise's long-waisted form moving with supple grace, Julie's body conveying a compact, vibrant energy. Denise's face was fixed, Julie's cheerfully bland.

The Trailsman set out when they were ready, and he soon found a stand of sweet wild plums and a cluster of raspberry bushes that made for a refreshing breakfast. He moved on, stayed in high land, and drew to a halt on a ridge that afforded a sweeping view of the land below.

It was easy enough to pick out the two groups of riders below and slightly behind. They were separated by a good half-mile, Reiber's group riding hard, Colson moving more carefully, still searching for him. Each concentrated on its own pursuit, still unaware of the other, though that wouldn't last through the day, Fargo felt certain. He turned and rode on with Denise alongside him, Julie a few paces behind, and the sun was in the afternoon sky when he halted to rest the horses. Julie stretched out on the grass near him, her round breasts pressed hard into the shirt and her round-cheeked, sweet face surveyed him from beneath the loose, pale-yellow hair.

"How long till we reach the Mesabi Range, Fargo?" she asked.

"Another two days maybe," he guessed, and she nodded thoughtfully.

"I've been thinking hard," Julie told him. "Have you decided what to do with me?"

"I guess the deciding is for you to do," Fargo said.

"May I have till tomorrow?" Julie asked.

"Why not?" Fargo shrugged. "We'll just keep enough distance from them." He rose, climbed onto the pinto, and set out again until the night came and he found a protected ledge. A small fire again warmed the beef jerky. He saw Denise watch Julie with long, studied glances, and he smiled inwardly. Julie was plainly still an enigma to her. It was after Julie prepared to bed down and changed into the loose pajamas that she came to sit beside him, the last embers of the fire barely flickering.

"I know what I want to do, Fargo," she said, and her hand rested on his arm. He saw Denise, some distance away, sit up at once. "It's all so silly and unnecessary," Julie began, and saw Fargo's frown. "I mean Tom and Uncle Cyrus down there competing with each other to find me, each one convinced he's the one I need. They both want to help me and it's time they stopped being so stubborn and foolish about it, and I'm going down and tell them both that."

"You're going to what?" Denise marveled.

"I'm going to get them to stop all this feuding. I'm going to get them to work together with me and for me," Julie said. "That's the way it ought to be, and I'll make them see that." She paused and her hand tightened ever so slightly on Fargo's arm. "With your help, and consent, of course," she said to him, blue eyes filled with intense sincerity.

"You don't need my help for that," he protested.

"But I do. I'll need it when I face them, to let them know that I mean exactly what I say and that I have you to back me up. And then I'll want you to help me try to find the map and the will."

"Then you'll be freezing both of them out," Fargo said.

"No, not at all. I'll make them understand that. But this way they won't be constantly at each other over who should help me and how. You'll help me, act as a neutral party. They'll actually prefer it, though they won't admit it," Julie said, and ended with a little laugh.

"You really think you can do this," Fargo asked her.

"Yes. You can do so much with caring and honesty and love," Julie said. "Will you help me? Soon as I find the silver, I'll be able to pay you whatever you want. Please, Fargo?"

He allowed a small laugh. "Why not? I've come this far. Might as well see it through," he said, casting a glance across at Denise. She sat staring at him, then flung herself back onto her blanket and turned her back to him.

"Thank you, Fargo," Julie half-whispered, and again she brushed his cheek with her Cupid's-bow mouth, fleeting sweetness. She rose, took her blanket, and set herself on the far end of the ledge.

Fargo took his bedroll and climbed on top of the rock protrusion, set his things out, and had just finished undressing when he heard the movement at the far end of the ledge. The Colt was in his hand and he was crouched in the trees when the form came into sight, nightdress swinging furiously as she strode along the top of the rock.

"Where the hell are you, Fargo?" she hissed, and he stepped from the trees. She spied him instantly and came toward him as he sat down on the bedroll. "Did you really swallow all that bilge?" Denise accused.

"Maybe it's not bilge. Maybe it's the best way of settling all this," Fargo said. "I think she might pull it off."

"Miss Sweetness and Light with her magic wand," Denise scoffed.

"You just don't understand her, honey," Fargo said, and there was no condemnation in his voice. "You've never met her kind of person."

"She's got a greedy, grasping uncle and a stepfather who can't wait to get his hands on that silver and maybe her little ass, too. And she's going to coat them all with love and goodness. You're damn right I don't understand it." Denise scowled. She halted her angry outburst and cocked her head to one side as she gave him a hard, piercing stare. "And I'm wondering about you buying it," she said.

"Wondering what?" he asked.

"Whether you've gone soft in the head or whether you've ideas of her being grateful enough to lay," Denise challenged.

"You really have a cynical outlook on everything," he said with a certain amount of wonder in his voice.

"It's called experience, the fruits of life," she returned.

"Sometimes you can take good things out of life and not just the bad. As for your question—no, I'm not thinking about laying her." He hadn't actually thought about it. Not much, anyway, he murmured silently. Passing, abstract thoughts didn't count.

"Good," Denise said. "You'd get all covered with syrup."

"Damn little hard-nose," Fargo muttered.

"Whatever," she said, yanking the nightgown off in one motion. She was atop him at once, her lips demanding, hungering. "Damn you, Fargo," she murmured, shifting to push one longish breast into his mouth. "Aaaaah, aaaah," she moaned as he pulled on it, letting his tongue tickle the soft-firm tip. She pressed her wiry black nap down against him as he rose, hardened with the touch of her, and when he thrust upward seeking her, she came down over him, descending so that she filled her soft, lubricious tunnel and rubbed against him. "Jesus, oh, oh . . . oooooh," Denise gasped out, her gossamer brown hair falling half over his face as her mouth found his. She was making love with a new urgency, using passion as an escape, anger as an ally to heightened ecstasy.

She moved against him, slowly first, then with a furious pumping. Her breast in his mouth jiggled as she came down hard against him, each time with a half-groan, half-grunt of pleasure. When their moment came for both of them, Denise arched her back for a long moment, sitting high atop him. Her entire body quivered and then she fell forward atop him, her breasts pressed into his face with wonderful softness. She trembled in ecstasy until, finally, with a groan of despair, her legs stretched out and she fell to her side against him.

He waited till her beige eyes opened and stared at him. "That's not going to change anything," he told her gently.

"I know that," she sniffed disdainfully. "But it'll help keep your mind off Miss Goodness." She rose, pulled the nightgown on, and walked from him without another word or another glance, her back held very straight.

He smiled, turned on his side, and realized she would probably never understand Julie Hudson.

He slept well and woke with the morning sun. When he gathered his things and dressed and returned down to the base of the rock protrusion, he saw Julie dressed and waiting for him with a warm, welcoming smile while Denise still brushed her hair. "Been thinking about how to do this," he said to Julie. "I'll let them see me, let them know you have backup, just in case you don't reach them the way you think you will."

"All right," she said. "But I'll reach them." She smiled with absolute, almost serene confidence and squeezed his hand for an instant.

Denise's voice interrupted. "What do I do, sell tickets?"

"I'd hope you'll be giving me all your support," Julie said evenly.

"That's me, your old spiritual guide," Denise grunted.

"Very well put," Julie said as she pulled onto her horse.

Fargo laughed quietly at Denise's glare of exasperation. He swung onto the Ovaro and led the way down the hillside, going north to meet their pursuers. They were still separate, he saw as he spotted the two groups. He continued downward until he found a flat rock that jutted out.

"You go out there and wait," he said to Julie. "They can't miss seeing you in a few minutes, and they'll both come charging this way." Julie nodded and moved her horse to stand at the very edge of the flat rock while Fargo stayed back in the trees with Denise. He cast a glance at her and saw she continued to view everything with a jaundiced eye. Yet she was also unable to mask her curiosity. Fargo returned his gaze to Julie and almost a half-hour had gone by when he heard her call out without looking back.

"They saw me," she said. "They've both changed direction and they're heading this way."

"Good. They'll be busy racing through the woods now. You come on back and we'll get ready for them when they arrive below." Again he led the way downward until he reached a spot where the land cleared away in a troughlike area that was only a dozen yards from the rock above. Again, he moved behind the first of the trees with Denise and unholstered the big Sharps. He waited, listening to the thunder of hoofbeats approaching.

Colson was the first to burst onto the cleared area and he leapt from his horse, rushed to Julie, and pulled her into his arms. "You got away. Goddamn, you got away," he said fervently, and turned from her as Cyrus Reiber and his men rode up. Reiber's eyes were on Julie as he swung from the saddle.

"Julie, girl," he called out, and rushed to her. She returned his hug with a warm embrace. "You send him packing?" Cyrus Reiber asked.

Julie stepped back a pace from both men. "No, I didn't get away and I didn't send him packing. He's here."

Fargo saw both men look from her instantly, a moment of something close to panic in their eyes as they glanced around the clearing. Fargo waited a second, then stepped from behind the tree, Denise following him, the big rifle raised to fire. "Right here, gents," he said. "Don't do anything dumb."

Colson was the first to recover and frown at Julie. "What is all this, Julie?"

"Fargo's here to make sure you listen to me without fighting among yourselves," she said. "I want all this feuding and fighting stopped right now." She managed to combine a firm, chastising tone with warmth and appeal, Fargo noted in admiration. "You're both being foolish. I love you both and you want to help me. So stop feuding and do it, together, all of us together. I'll never be able to remember anything if I'm thinking about you fighting over who has the right to help me and who's best for me. It's just not right, Tom. It's all wrong, Cyrus. Love and caring isn't something you can divide up like slices of a pie. It embraces everything."

Fargo saw Colson and Cyrus Reiber exchange quick sheepish glances.

"I want you with me, both of you, I need you both here with me," Julie went on. "Not fighting but giving me all your support, all your love and caring. That's what you've been doing in your own ways all these years. This is no time to stop."

Fargo watched her reach out both hands, put one over Colson's hand and the other over Reiber's. She guided their hands toward each other. "Please," she said. "Don't make me do this alone, without your love and caring by my side." She touched their hands together and it was Cyrus Reiber who gave in first, opened his palm to shake hands.

"Hell, since you put it that way," he said. "Besides, I never could say no to you, Julie, even when you were a little girl."

"I guess it is the best way," Tom Colson said, grasping Cyrus's hand.

Julie hugged them both to her, and when she turned away, her face was wreathed in a wide smile.

"She did it," Fargo said. "She did it."

"I'll be damned," Denise muttered.

Fargo glanced at her. "You convinced that it works, sometimes?" he asked. "In the right hands it works."

"No," Denise snapped.

"Dammit, what do you need to convince you?" He frowned. "You just saw it in front of your own eyes."

Julie's voice interrupted any answer Denise might have had. "Fargo, come on down please," she said, and he walked forward as Denise waited a moment before hurrying after him. "Fargo's going to help me find the map and the will," Julie said, which drew immediate frowns from Reiber and Colson.

"You said we were going to do that," Reiber protested.

"No, I said I wanted you here with me, giving me your love and caring and spiritual support," Julie corrected. "But I can't do it if I have to keep wondering whose feelings I'm hurting by one thing or another. This way it'll be simpler and better. We can all work together, care together, and find what we want together. That's the way it ought to be."

"One big happy family," Denise commented.

"That's right," Julie said, refusing to be bothered by Denise's unfailing cynicism.

"I'll be happier when I get the money you owe me, Colson," Denise said. "Let's have it."

"I don't have it with me," Colson said.

"Then take up a collection. I want it now," Denise growled. "I'm here for my money, not this love feast."

"I'm sure Julie will advance it to me when we find the silver," Colson said stiffly, the cold handsomeness in his face quick to reassert itself.

"Of course," Julie said. "Just be patient a little longer, Denise."

"Do I have a choice?" Denise sniffed.

"I guess not," Julie said apologetically. "Try being part of us. That'll help. I'd like that."

"I always try better after I get paid," Denise returned.

Julie shrugged and walked to her horse. She took in Cyrus Reiber and Tom Colson with one glance. "The Mesabi Range is waiting," she said, and the two men quickly climbed onto their horses. Julie swung between them as they rode off. Colson's men and Reiber's followed, keeping to themselves while they exchanged wary and somewhat confused glances.

Fargo turned the pinto south and stayed riding at the outside of the others, and Denise came alongside him.

"You just saw something unusual and you just can't believe it, that's your problem," he told her.

"I know what I saw. It's what I didn't see that bothers me," Denise tossed back.

"What's that mean?" Fargo asked.

"We'll talk tonight," she said as Julie turned to beckon to Fargo.

He spurred his pinto forward and caught up to where Julie rode between Reiber and Colson.

"You're the Trailsman, Fargo. We'll follow you," she said.

He nodded and rode forward with Denise's words still rattling around in his mind.

6

Fargo set a fast pace through the day with only a few short stops to rest the horses. When night drew near, he sent one of Colson's men out to bring down a quail or a grouse and one of Reiber's to do the same in the other direction. Both were successful, bringing back two birds apiece, and Fargo called a halt to the day's riding early enough to allow time to pluck the birds and begin the cooking.

Over dinner, Colson's men and Reiber's began to mingle with careful wariness while Julie sat with her uncle and stepfather during the meal.

When it was over and Denise had gone into the trees to change for bed, Julie came to him and took his hands in hers. "You going to say I told you so?" He grinned.

"No, I'm going to say we'll have a lot of time to work together. I'll like that. You've been the only one to believe in me all along. That helped more than you know."

"I'm glad, then," Fargo said. He wondered if she realized the strangely powerful combination of vibrations she sent out, altruistic, lofty sentiments along with very personal, vibrant ones.

"Believing always helps," Julie said. She squeezed both his hands in hers before turning to hurry off to the other side of the camp.

The others had mostly settled down and Fargo saw Julie take a spot near Cyrus Reiber and Tom Colson.

The Trailsman pulled his bedroll from the Ovaro and, as was his habit, started back into the trees beyond the campsite when he saw Denise hurrying after him in the long nightdress, blanket in hand.

"I don't feel like sleeping here," she said.

"You come with me and you're going to sleep and nothing else," he told her. "It's been a hard day's ride and it'll be a harder one tomorrow."

"Fine with me. Little Miss Goodness can hold your hand again tomorrow."

"Aren't we sharp-eyed," Fargo grunted as he set his bedroll down between two wide, old bitternut trees.

"Always," she said.

"Now you want to tell me what you meant this afternoon about the things you didn't see?" Fargo said. "Or was it that you really don't want to see what you did?"

"Oh, I saw all that kiss-and-be-happy love feast," she retorted disdainfully. "But Little Miss Goodness was the only one I saw who was happy."

"Meaning what?"

"She had Reiber and Colson in a corner, so they went along for their own reasons, not because she swept them up with all that love-and-caring shit."

"You just can't understand it, can you?" Fargo said with more sympathy than annoyance. "Your world has been too harsh and bitter for you to understand someone like Julie Hudson. You can't comprehend that special quality of sincerity, goodness, and caring she gives out. You can't believe that people respond to that, but they do."

"Pardon me while I throw up," Denise snorted.

"Said it once and I'll say it again: you envy her. You wish you could feel the way she does about people. You'd like to trust more and believe more, but you can't and you envy someone who can," Fargo said.

"She's certainly made you a believer."

"I just appreciate something rare when I see it."

"I don't trust anybody that's all good," Denise grunted, and lay down on her blanket. "They're either saints or swindlers, and I'm not comfortable around either."

"Hard-nose," Fargo grunted as he stretched out on his bedroll. "Go to sleep."

"Yes, sir," she sniffed.

Fargo smiled as he closed his eyes. She was past changing, her protective shell too hardened, he sighed, and went to sleep.

The night was a quiet time and he woke with the new day, washed, dressed, and waited for Denise to join him as he returned to the camp. The others were mostly ready, and Julie tossed him a smile bright as the new sun. She had changed into a dark-brown riding skirt and shirt that made her pale-yellow hair more luminous than usual.

"We'll be riding hard. I want to make the Mesabi in the next two days," Fargo said as he swung onto the Ovaro. Denise came in just behind him as he set out and he saw Julie riding between Colson and Reiber while the others followed in straggly groups.

Fargo kept to his word and set a hard pace, pausing only to water the horses. When dusk came, he chose a narrow dip in the land to camp. Julie, for all her delicate coloring, seemed the freshest of anyone as she helped build a fire to warm the remainder of the birds shot the day before. Darkness descended and the meal was taken, Denise sitting beside him. Julie ate with her uncle and stepfather, chattering away with seemingly endless energy.

Fargo's eyes swept the others and came to a pause where one of Colson's hands—a short, squat man with a squat face—and one of Reiber's men—rangy and thin of build—sat together and apart from the others. They concentrated on their private, murmured conversation, and Fargo heard Denise's voice at his elbow.

"Soul mates?" she grunted derisively.

"I've noticed they've been very chummy all day," Fargo said.

"Sort-of a sudden friendship, isn't it?" Denise said.

Fargo smiled. "You think they're hatching something," he said. "The thought passed through my mind, too. They're hired-on scum with no real loyalty to anyone."

"What are you going to do?"

"Wait."

"Wait? That's all? Just wait?" Denise said.

"There are all kinds of ways to wait," Fargo said, and he rose, took his bedroll from the pinto, and heard Julie's voice as he passed near her.

"Good night," she called out, and he waved back and returned to where Denise waited. He let the camp settle down, made a quick count of the figures stretched out on the ground. They were all there, he noted, and he started to climb the tree-covered slope that bordered the dip of land.

Denise stepped from the shadows, her blanket under one arm.

"You stay in camp," he said.

"I don't feel like it."

He considered a moment and then strode on. "All right, but you do what I tell you to do."

"What's that going to be?" she asked crossly as he set his bedroll down at a spot where the slope leveled off and a sugar maple rose high.

"You get some sleep and stay here."

She frowned. "Where are you going?"

"I don't know if those two are up to something or not. And if they are, I don't know what. I'm going to try to be in more than one place at one time," he said.

"You're not making any damn sense, Fargo."

"You want to help me? Then bed down here and stay here. I don't want to be worrying about where you are," Fargo said.

"All right," she grumbled, and began to settle down on her blanket.

Fargo walked from the big sugar maple to vanish in the night. He continued on another dozen yards before halting to peer up at the trees that surrounded him. He chose a wide-spreading, thickly branched box elder and began to pull himself up into the tree, climbing until he was high enough to see the campsite in one direction and the sugar maple where Denise slept in her blanket. He scanned the sleeping figures in the camp, counted, and grunted in satisfaction. They were all in place. If the two men had planned anything, he had the feeling it would be against Julie, an attempt to take her and whatever she might remember for themselves. He found a more comfortable crook in the branch and draped himself across it to settle in to wait.

But the wait wasn't long: Fargo suddenly saw two of the prone shapes rise, move with quick, stealthy steps. He leaned forward on the branch, ready to swing to the ground, but felt the furrow slide across his brow. The two figures were not moving toward where Julie lay wrapped in her blanket. Instead, they crept away from the campsite and into the trees at the edge of the slope. Following the dark shapes in the weak moonlight, the Trailsman watched them turn, move toward where he hung in the tree. They spread out and came forward, and he saw them obviously peering through the dark wooded slope, searching as they went. They passed beneath him, not more than a half-dozen yards from the big box elder, and he watched them continue forward. They searched for where he had bedded down, he realized with surprise. He swung silently down through the tree, dropping to the ground on the balls of his feet.

He hurried forward, caught sight of the two figures again as they reached the spot where Denise lay asleep. Fargo, his brow still furrowed, unholstered the Colt and crept forward, the six-gun leveled and ready to bark.

The two figures halted at the sugar maple, closed together for a whispered exchange, and moved forward again.

Fargo followed, halting as they reached Denise. He saw her instincts bring her awake as she sat bolt-upright and found herself staring into the barrel of the revolver held by the squat-figured man.

"Where is he?" the man rasped. "We watched him come up this way and you went with him. Now, where is he?"

"I don't know," Denise said honestly.

The man's hand shot out and seized her by the front of the nightgown, twisted the garment as he pulled her forward. "I said where is he, dammit?" he snarled.

"I don't know, I told you," Denise returned.

"One more time, girlie, or we break your skull," the man threatened.

"He said he was going to be in more than one place at the same time," Denise answered, and received a slap across the face.

"No smart-ass answers," the squat figure hissed. "Where is he?"

Fargo took a step forward. "Right here," he said quietly. Both men spun in surprise, but the squat one kept his hold on Denise. "Let her go," Fargo said. The thin, rangy one yanked his gun from its holster and the other man dived into the trees, taking Denise along with him. Fargo fired and the thin one arched backward through the air as the shot tore through his body.

Fargo was already dropping low as the two shots from the trees hurtled over his head. In a crouch, he darted forward and heard the man dragging himself and Denise through the brush. Suddenly there was an oath of pain from the man. "Goddamn, bitch," he swore, and Fargo heard the quick sounds of someone fleeing through the brush. Denise had torn from his grasp. Probably she'd kicked him in the groin. Fargo smiled grimly and moved forward more quickly. He glimpsed the short, squat figure, the man crouched, hesitating for an instant, uncertain whether to try to chase after Denise or not.

"Drop the gun," Fargo called out. His answer was two more shots that hurtled past him as the man dropped low and fired. Fargo held return fire. It would be easy enough to kill him, he knew, but he wanted some answers.

He moved forward again, a quick motion that brought him behind a tree as the man fired again, the shot wide and off the mark. He had only one shot left, Fargo counted, and then his wild-creature hearing caught the sound of bullets being pushed into a chamber. He was reloading.

Fargo whirled from behind the tree and fired four shots, all aimed to fly just over the grass and catch the man in the legs. One hit its mark and Fargo heard the man's cry of pain and glimpsed the squat figure fall sideways.

"Jesus, damn," the man cried out.

"Drop the gun while you still can do it," Fargo said from a crouch.

"All right, all right, my ankle's broke," the man called out.

"Throw your gun out here," Fargo ordered, and the revolver, an old Smith & Wesson single-action rim-fire with a plated brass frame, flew from the bushes to land in the grass. Fargo stepped past it as he straightened, the Colt ready to fire, and saw the man half on his side, one leg drawn up, his face contorted in pain. The Trailsman holstered the Colt and stepped to the man, saw the blood staining his ankle. "You've some explaining to do, mister," Fargo growled.

"Help me straighten my leg out first. The pain's killing me," the man said as he lay half on his side.

Fargo knelt down, reached out, and started to carefully pull the man's leg when the figure whirled and he had only a split second to see the length of rotted log hurtling straight at his face. He ducked his head and took the blow full on the top of his forehead as the man rammed the piece of wood straight forward.

Fargo felt the explosion of pain, and his head became a place of flashing red and yellow lights. He toppled back and onto his side, shook his head, and the flashing lights ceased for a half-second, long enough for him to see the short, squat figure manage to propel itself onto him, dragging the shattered ankle behind. The lights returned, bursting inside his head as he fell backward, and he felt the man's hands yanking at the big Colt in its holster. He shook his head again as, fighting out of instinct, he reached one hand down and closed it around the man's arm as the Colt came out of the holster. The flashing lights blinked out and Fargo saw his opponent trying to pull his arm free, the Colt in his hand.

The exploding lights returned, though less bright now, a dull series of flashes, and Fargo managed to keep the squat figure in sight. He twisted the arm and the man cried out in pain but from his ankle as it took the weight of his body. Shaking off the last of the lights in his head, Fargo pushed himself to one knee just as the man managed to pull his arm free. The man started to lift the gun to fire at point-blank range from a half-sitting position when Fargo's arm shot out, his flattened, stiff palm slamming into the man's elbow with all his weight behind it. The man fired just as his arm was knocked back and downward, and Fargo saw the surprise and pain flood the squat face.

The man's eyes widened, his mouth fell open with a guttural, gasping sound, and Fargo's glance dropped down to see the shot had plunged into the man's lower belly. A widening stain of red spread across his groin and the man continued to make hollow gasping noises, his wide eyes staring emptily into space, until he fell forward not unlike a sitting statue being knocked over. The Colt fell onto the ground and Fargo scooped it up and pushed to his feet, nudged the crumpled figure with the toe of his boot. It moved with lifeless flaccidity.

The throbbing in his head was still there, though less intense, as Fargo turned away and swore silently. There'd be no questions answered. He whirled, the Colt in his hand at once, as he heard the brush move. The figure rose, nightgown draped around its supple long-waisted form.

"You all right?" Denise asked, concern in her voice as she came toward him. "I saw part of it."

"My head hurts, but I guess I'm lucky for it," Fargo said.

"Where were you when they came to me?" she asked.

"Watching, wondering what they were going to do," Fargo said. "They took me by surprise. I expected they'd be going after Julie."

"They definitely wanted you."

"Get your blanket. We'll go back to camp. They'll have heard the shots and be up and wondering," Fargo said.

"This ought to be interesting," Denise commented as she followed Fargo down the slope.

When he reached the campsite, he found everyone awake and on their feet, as he expected.

Julie was the first to rush forward to him. "Thank goodness you're all right," she said. "I heard the shots, woke, and saw you were gone."

Fargo's eyes went past her to Reiber and Colson. "Two of the men decided to come gunning for me," Fargo said. "One of your boys, Cyrus, and one of yours, Colson."

"That'd be Hank Eamons, he's not here," Reiber said.

"And Steve Crater. He's the only one of my men missing," Colson said.

"Got any ideas on it?" Fargo asked.

"First, they were old friends. Of course, neither Tom nor I knew that when we hired them. Seems they used to herd together. They spent most of today riding together," Reiber said.

"I know that," Fargo said laconically.

"It might have all been my fault," Reiber said. "They were listening when I told Tom I'd paid you a goodly sum to bring Julie to me. I guess they decided to relieve you of the money and cut out together. I guess I owe you an apology, Fargo."

"Include me in. I'm just glad you were ready for them," Colson said.

"It's called having a suspicious nature," Fargo said.

"I'm certainly glad for that," Julie said, and gave him a quick embrace. "Now let's all get back to sleep."

"Be ready to ride early," Fargo warned. He had started up the slope from camp when Denise caught up to him.

"Don't tell me you're buying that explanation," she said.

"It's possible enough," Fargo said.

"Sure it's possible. Only I don't believe a damn word of it," Denise threw back.

"What do you believe?" Fargo asked.

"Those two were working on orders from Colson and Reiber. You're in their way now. Get rid of you and they'd have Julie to themselves again. Maybe they decided to make a deal between themselves," Denise said.

"I won't rule it out, but I can't go around accusing them because of your suspicions. Besides, it failed, whoever was behind it. I don't expect any more trouble."

"Always look on the bright side? Taking a page from Miss Goodness? She's sure made a disciple of you," Denise sniffed with disdain.

"It's not being a disciple. It's experience. It's knowing when people back away. It's knowing not to waste important time," he said. "Now get some sleep, dammit."

She lay down and he fetched his bedroll and her blanket, and the rest of the night was still. Morning came too soon, but he saw to it that they were riding before the sun fully crested the low hills. Again, he set a hard pace and they reached the Mesabi with the late day's sun.

Julie didn't wait for him to motion to her as she moved her horse forward to come alongside him. "We'll be riding together from here on," she said brightly, and Denise pulled back disdainfully.

Fargo slowed and his eyes swept the land that stretched before him, sharp, high crags, ravines, and gulleys, not a lot of tree cover, sandstone gorges, and the craggy terrain dotted with the entrances of abandoned iron-ore mines. He glanced at Julie and saw her eyes were narrowed as she stared out across the Mesabi. "You remembering anything?" he asked.

"Deeper," she murmured. "We went in much deeper, all the way to those high crags in the distance."

"We can make them tomorrow. We'll make camp somewhere along here." Fargo led the way forward till he found a flat place between two abandoned mines. "This'll do," he said as his gaze went from one boarded entranceway to the other. He let Julie dismount and watched her stare up at the old mines and saw the tiny furrow touch her brow. "They're familiar, aren't they?" he said.

"Only in general. I remember seeing them, one after the other," Julie said.

"He told you the will and the map was in one of them, didn't he?" Fargo pressed.

Julie's furrow became a frown and her face drew together as she pressed her eyes tightly shut. "Maybe, maybe," she breathed. "I'm not sure." She opened her eyes to stare at him. "I need more to help me remember. We have to go in deeper."

"Tomorrow," Fargo said, turning from her as the dark began to descend. "Get some sleep," he said, certain that the exhausting day's ride would see to that.

The night came quickly and he felt the tiredness pull at his own body. Denise set her blanket down at the edge of the space and pulled it around herself. Fargo put his bedroll nearby, undressed, and stretched out. "There's no reason for you to have your nose out of joint," he murmured, just loud enough for her to hear.

"My nose isn't out of joint. I just don't want to interfere with your helping Little Miss Goodness get her memory back," Denise tossed at him.

"The sooner she does, the sooner you get your money, so don't knock it," Fargo answered.

"Heaven forbid," she said tartly, and Fargo stayed silent. He understood her, but he wasn't about to indulge her in her fits of envy and jealousy. He turned on his side, closed his eyes, and was asleep in minutes.

7

In the morning, Fargo found a small stream that trickled down the dry stones with enough force to let everyone wash and water the horses. He rode on then with Julie beside him. He saw her eyes sweeping the hills and the abandoned-mine openings that dotted the terrain. "Anything familiar?" he asked.

"Everything and nothing," Julie said. "I remember the Mesabi well. I always kept the memory of the mine entrances. Many were abandoned even back then. But we have to go in deeper."

Fargo nodded and increased the pace as he moved across a long, flat ledge of land; it ended in a hilly stretch that leveled off again, this time in a plateau that held a modest stand of red mulberry. He reined to a halt to let everyone enjoy the fruit, and saw the excitement in Julie's face.

"I remember this place. We stopped here, too, and breakfasted on the berries."

"Keep digging," Fargo urged.

"I will," she said as he led the way on and rode until the long shadows began to cross the craggy, hilly terrain. He spotted two thin white-tailed deer and sent four of the men after them. When he reached the end of the plateau, he called a halt and saw the men returning with the two deer.

"Anything else come to you?" he asked Julie.

"No." She frowned. "When I try too hard, everything seems to go blank."

"Happens often. The mind doesn't like giving up its inner thoughts," Fargo said.

"But I feel things are familiar. I feel there are memories just waiting to jump out but I can't free them," Julie said.

"Don't force it," Fargo said. "Relax, have supper, and things will come to you." He dismounted and helped the others skin the two deer and build a makeshift spit and a fire. The game was roasting before night came, and the meal was finally ready for eating.

Denise nodded to him with cool formality and he made no attempt to draw her out. It was best, he decided, to let her come out of her moods by herself. When the meal was finally finished, the remaining meat was cut away to save and the fires put out.

Julie came to him then in her loose pajamas. "Sleep beside me tonight, Fargo. My mind is racing with bits and pieces of memory, everything all mixed up. It may come together while I sleep. Sleep does that sometimes, you know."

"Yes, I've experienced that myself," he said.

"If I wake up remembering anything I want you there to hear it."

"Fair enough." He pushed to his feet and walked to the pinto for his bedroll. Denise was nearby and he paused at her. "Sleep well," he said, and received a smile of acid tolerance. He watched her take her things to the far end of the campsite while he settled down nearby.

Julie soon came toward him with her blanket. She set it down not more than a foot from his, and he enjoyed the way her full little rear filled the loose pajamas and her high, round breasts briefly pushed hard against the top as she settled down.

"Good night, Fargo," she said, her tinkly voice softly clear.

" 'Night," he murmured, and closed his eyes to let sleep replenish his tired body. Most of the night had passed when his wild-creature hearing caught the sound beside him; his eyes snapped open, his hand on the butt of the big Colt at his side, and he saw Julie half-sitting, blinking, staring into the night. He pushed up on one elbow and she half-turned to him, her eyes very round, her voice a half-whisper.

"A very high, steep, steep trail, a terrible, dangerous trail," she breathed. "Very narrow, rock at one side and a terrible drop on the other." She halted and her breasts heaved against the pajama top as she drew in deep breaths.

"You're sure?"

"Yes, yes, I remember it clearly now. We climbed it all the way to the top. It all exploded inside me just now."

"Good, very good," Fargo said. "We'll talk more about it in the morning."

"Why am I shaking so?" Julie asked.

"Nerves. Tension. Just a reaction."

She fell back onto the blanket but her hand reached out to close over his. He held her hand as he lay down again also, and she kept her hand in his until she fell asleep and he felt her hand relax, grow limp, and fall from his. He drew his arm back and let himself return to sleep until the new day arrived.

He woke first, and as he waited for the others to gather themselves and for Julie and Denise to change into riding clothes, his eyes sought out Colson and Reiber. "You keep riding east, along the passages between the hills. I'm going on ahead to do some searching. I'll find you later," he said.

"You want me to come along?" Julie asked.

"No, I'll make better time alone," he told her, and

109

sent the Ovaro into a fast canter. He rode from sight quickly, headed down side passages and up small trails, and slowed after a spell while his eyes continued to scan the high crags that rose up, half bearing the boards of abandoned-mine entrances. He continued till noon, then halted to rest the horse.

When he went on, his gaze was fixed on a distant row of steep craggy hills that rose much higher than any he had passed. As he drew closer, he saw that the Mesabi rose in two levels, the second one higher than the first with its own hills and stone formations. He rode closer and passed below the first set of hills, which rose up almost perpendicular to the trail he rode. He scanned their steep sides, but they held no passages and he went on. The second level of the range was set back from the lower one, as though a giant hand had placed one atop the other with a set-back for the upper one.

Fargo had gone perhaps another hour when he slowed and felt the excitement stab at him. A high, steep side of rock rose up; it curved along one side where a very narrow trail hugged the clifflike formation. The other side of the narrow, curving trail was a sheer drop to rocks some hundred feet below, he saw as he dismounted and peered over the edge. He scanned the narrow trail that led up in a slow curve against the towering side of rock. It was barely wide enough for one horse at a time, he noted, but it fit Julie's description perfectly. His eyes narrowed as he peered upward. The top of the narrow trail curved out of his sight and he decided against trying to go up. Exploring could wait until he showed it to Julie.

He turned, rode back the way he had come, but this time his gaze searched the paths below and he paused once to examine a half-dozen unshod pony prints. They were old, the edges crumbled, and he hurried on. There'd be only a few scouting parties venturing in the Mesabi, he was certain. This was not country that attracted Indians. It was neither good hunting nor good raiding country.

Fargo returned to the saddle and hurried on until he spotted the small plume of dry dust to his left. He changed directions and rode until he came in sight of the riders, Julie's pale-yellow hair glistening in the sun. He rode onto an open high ledge and let the others see him as he beckoned to them. Julie led the way as they changed direction at once and reached him some twenty minutes later.

"Found something for you to look at," he said, and this time Julie was beside him as he turned the pinto around and headed east through the hills. The others followed and were only a hundred yards behind when he reached the high stone rise with the narrow, curving trail around the one side.

Julie stared at it, her eyes growing wide.. "You found it! That's it. My God, that's it." She swung to the ground and walked closer to the narrow, curved trail as the others came up to halt and dismount.

"You remember where it leads at the top?" Fargo asked.

"Only that there were more hills and more abandoned mines," she said. "But that's it! I'm so excited." She whirled and embraced Tom Colson and then Cyrus Reiber.

"Anything else come to you now?" Fargo pressed.

"No, not now, but I'm sure once we're at the top there'll be more to jog my memory," Julie said happily.

Fargo's eyes went to the narrow, curving passage and the sheer drop along the edge. "Don't count chickens yet," he muttered. "The first step is to get to the top alive. That's not going to be easy." His eyes went to the steep, curved passage again. "Wait here," he said, and walked to beginning of the trail. He began to walk along the narrow curve, measuring the width

111

with his eyes as he peered upward. It appeared to stay pretty much the same width, he decided, and he paused frequently to rub his hands along the soil that covered the stone beneath. Finally he turned and walked back to where the others waited. He had gone only a small distance along the narrow path, but he had seen enough.

"Well?" Colson asked.

"I'll go up first. I expect I'll be able to see you down here from the top. When I wave, you start up. But the way it curves means you'll be out of sight for the middle part of the climb so listen carefully now," Fargo said. "First, you take it real slow. The topsoil is dry and loose. Everyone going up together could loosen it too much. You'll go up two at a time with a three-minute wait between each two." They nodded and he cast another glance at the narrow path. "Most important of all, there's no room for playing hero. You're each on your own. Anything happens to the person in front or behind you, there's no way you can help without going over yourself."

"I'm sure we'll make it just fine," Julie said.

"Love and goodness will see us through," Denise chimed in with mocking cheerfulness.

Fargo shot her a hard glance she shrugged off. "I'll go first. You follow me, Julie."

"No, I don't want that," Julie said, and he turned with surprise. "Everyone's taken enough risks to help me. I want to see everyone safely at the top first. Then I'll go up with Uncle Cy." She turned to Reiber with a warm smile. "All right?"

"Sure thing, Julie," Cyrus Reiber agreed.

"All right," Fargo said. "Denise will follow me. The rest of you pair off and wait till I signal down to you." He strode to the pinto and climbed into the saddle.

Denise followed after him only to halt as he paused at the foot of the narrow, curving ledge. She peered down over the edge and shuddered.

"That's your last look down," he said gruffly. "Concentrate on keeping your horse slow and calm. Keep stroking its neck. It'll sense the danger and start to get nervous. It's your job, and your neck, to keep it calm. No slowing down and no speeding up. Keep a steady pace."

"What if it goes wrong? What if it stumbles or loses footing and goes over?" Denise asked.

"Throw yourself sideways against the rock wall and hope you'll drop down on the ledge," Fargo said.

"Let's get started," Denise said, her face taking on tight-lipped determination.

Fargo cast a glance back at Julie, who blew him a kiss with a wave. He took the pinto up along the narrow curving ledge, and as he set a slow, steady climb, his eyes constantly checked the loose gravel and dirt that covered the ledge. He risked half-turning to glance back at Denise. She was some ten yards behind and holding the horse's reins in a white-knuckled grip.

"Relax," he called back to her. "Ease up. Keep your horse calm and let him pick his way."

She nodded and Fargo turned back to concentrate on his own riding. The curve around the side of the stone was both steeper and sharper than it had seemed from below, but it was negotiable. Only a mistake of judgment or a lapse into carelessness would bring death. A careful, steady ride would bring them through, he saw, and supremely confident in the Ovaro's footing, he half-turned in the saddle again to glance back at Denise. She was still there, still coming, and she hadn't made the mistake of trying to catch up, he saw with satisfaction. Maybe Denise wasn't a great rider but her hard-nosed determination would see her through. He smiled to himself and took the pinto up the last of the long curve.

The wall of stone continued to rise up to his right,

but he saw the narrow pathway widen and the flat ledge on top as the stone wall suddenly ended. He reached it and felt the perspiration in his own palms as he let the reins drop over the pinto's neck. He halted, turned the horse, and watched Denise come around the last of the long curve and finally draw up alongside him. Her face glistened with little beads of sweat and her shirt was wet and clung to her breasts. She slid from the horse and sank to one knee on the ground, her eyes peering down at the gorge below. "God, I don't want to do that again," she breathed. "I'm wrung out."

"You did well," Fargo said. He walked the Ovaro past the top of the stone, moved along the ledge, and found a spot that let him see down to where the others waited below. They appeared terribly small and much farther down than he'd expected. He climbed onto a rock and waved both arms until they spotted him and he saw Julie's pale-yellow hair move as she waved back. He raised one arm and made a sweeping motion. Two figures left his sight as they started up the narrow ledge. He moved, glimpsed them as they began to get into the bottom of the long curve, and then the high rock wall obscured further sight of them. He returned to Denise and found her standing beside her horse, using the water from her canteen to wash her face and neck.

Her beige eyes studied him as he relaxed against a rock. "You changed your mind about what you promised when this is over?" she asked.

"What was that?"

"About our staying together for a while?"

"No, I haven't changed my mind. Why?"

"You're getting so chummy with little Julie," Denise sniffed.

"I'm doing what needs doing, that's all," Fargo

said. "You mind your manners and we'll have that time together."

She accepted the reply but with reservations in her eyes.

Fargo pushed to his feet and walked to the top of the narrow ledge as the first rider appeared. It was Colson, he saw, the man's face strained. One of his men rode behind him. "Goddamn, that takes the hide off a man's nerves," Colson said when he reached the top and the flat ground. The other man just sat in the saddle with his head bowed as he took in deep gulps of air.

"Sit down. It'll be a long wait before they're all up here," Fargo said. He leaned against the curved, wind-blown trunk of a small alder and waited. The next two riders were two of Reiber's men and the next two were Colson's hands. When the next two pairs arrived, the shadows were beginning to lengthen.

"Reiber and the girl are next," one of the men said.

Fargo nodded and his eyes swept the sky.

Denise quickly saw the frown that touched his brow. "What is it?" she asked.

He grunted a laugh. There was little she missed. "Those clouds mean rain, maybe a lot of it," he said.

"Tonight?" she questioned.

"Early tomorrow sometime, I'd guess," Fargo said.

"I wouldn't mind a little cooling rain," Denise said.

"This could be a lot more than that," Fargo answered. "A hard, steady rain will be dangerous up here. There's a lot of loose soil and soft clay along with these rocks. It'll turn into mud pretty damn quick, and these hills and gulleys are made for mudslides."

He had just cast another glance at the clouds when the scream exploded from below, another wailing sound mixed in with it. "Goddamn," Fargo swore as he spun around. The scream came again, Julie's voice filled with terror as it spiraled up alongside the stone wall of the ledge. The scream continued, became a high-pierced wail that finally subsided to a dim plaintive cry. Fargo saw the fearful, shocked panic in Tom Colson's face. "Everybody stays here," Fargo said as he ran for the ledge and started down on foot.

The whimpering cries continued to drift up and he cursed again as he carefully half-ran, half-strode down the narrow ledge. If she were hanging on to the edge with her fingertips, he'd never reach her in time, he knew, unless Cyrus Reiber was somehow clinging to her. He fought down the impulse to run faster, aware that a slip could send him over the edge.

The curve seemed endless and then suddenly he saw her, still in the saddle, both hands pressed against the stone wall as if she were a supplicant praying at a wailing wall. The horse remained unmoving, he saw gratefully, and he slowed to a walk as he approached the animal. He saw Julie's round-cheeked face pulled tight with terror and anguish, and her eyes darted to the edge of the narrow path. He glanced down to the rocks far below and saw Cyrus Reiber's shattered body a few feet from the lifeless carcass of his horse.

Fargo brought his eyes back to Julie as, with a slow, careful step, he reached the horse and took hold of the horse's cheek strap. "Take your hands from the wall," he said softly, putting confidence into his voice. She only stared back and stayed in position. "Take them down," he said again slowly, and she pulled her hands from the stone. "Put them on the saddle horn," he said, and she obeyed, her round blue eyes staring at him. "Now sit still and tell me what happened?"

"I was last," she said. "Everything seemed to be going well when it all happened, in a split second, right before my eyes. His horse slipped and went over the edge before Uncle Cyrus could do a thing. It took him right over with it." She halted and a low sobbing sound fell from her lips.

"Throw me the reins," Fargo said, and she tossed the straps to him. "You just keep sitting very straight in the saddle. You keep your balance and the horse will keep his," he added with more confidence than he felt. Turning carefully, he began to back his way up the narrow ledge, gently pulling the horse along with him. It seemed hours, though it was only minutes when, his eyes watching the horse's every step, he finally reached the top of the path and again felt the perspiration coating his palms.

Julie fell into Tom Colson's grasp as he lowered her from the saddle, and the others listened as she again told what had happened. Colson let her sink down on a flat stone, her hands held to her face as she sobbed.

Fargo lifted his eyes to scan the nearby terrain as the twilight began to lower. "Up there," he said, and pointed to a place between two hills of clay and stone where the land formed a kind of rolling cradle. "Bring her," he said to Colson, and swung onto the pinto and led the way to the spot. Denise swung from her horse near him and he cast her a hard glance. "No more smart remarks?" he pushed at her.

"Guess not," she said, and turned away.

A pall of silence hung over the others as night fell and they divided the rest of the deer meat over a small fire. Julie sat alone, knees drawn up and her arms clasped around her legs.

Fargo let the others finish the meal before he went to her and sat down beside her. Julie's round-cheeked face lifted to meet his eyes and her arms came up to encircle his neck.

"There wasn't anything you could do," he told her softly.

She drew back and peered deep into his eyes. "I

117

keep thinking maybe if I'd acted quicker, maybe I could've saved him."

"No," Fargo said firmly. "All you'd have done is go over with him. There was no room there. I told you that. You've got to put that out of your mind."

Her fingers dug into his arms. "Stay with me tonight, Fargo. I need to be with someone strong. I need to borrow strength," Julie said.

"I will," he promised. "Get your things together." She nodded and he helped her to her feet and watched her go behind one of the few alders in the area and emerge in the loose pajamas. She set her blanket against one edge of the campsite and Fargo took his bedroll from the Ovaro to see Denise nearby, a cool appraisal in her eyes. "Don't say anything you'll be sorry for," Fargo muttered.

"Wouldn't think of it," Denise returned.

"Don't you think she needs some comfort and support after what she's been through?" he asked with annoyance.

"I'm just wondering what happened to her stepdaddy, Colson. After all, he's been a father to her all these years," Denise said.

"Maybe he's not the right man for now," Fargo said. "Maybe he never was. That's not my concern. She's been through a terrible experience, seeing her uncle go that way. She wants me to stay with her, and I'll do it."

"Hold down the comforting," Denise said, and turned away.

"It's not like that," he tossed back, and strode across the camp to set his bedroll down beside Julie.

She turned at once, no hand in his this time but her warm, compact little body pressed tight against him. "Just stay with me, Fargo, just be here beside me with your strength," she murmured, pleading in her voice.

"Easy, now. Just relax," he said softly. "I'm here and I'm going to stay here."

She made a satisfied sound and settled against him, the pale-yellow hair brushing his face. In moments she was asleep, he realized with surprise, her even breathing a contented sound.

Fargo blew breath through his lips. He'd never be able to understand any of them, he murmured to himself. They were all the same: a puzzle wrapped in a mystery. He grunted and let himself fall asleep.

8

Julie was pulled hard against him when he woke with the morning, still sleeping peacefully. She looked little-girl-like with the pale-yellow hair framing her round-cheeked face. She stirred as he slid from beside her, but her eyes remained closed and he rose to gaze up at the sky. He swore under his breath. It was a lead-gray sky, solid with rain about to descend. He dressed and heard Julie as she woke and sat up. She focused on him and a warm, grateful smile touched the Cupid's-bow mouth at once.

"Thank you," she murmured. "You don't know how much your being with me helped."

"I'm glad," he said, and pulled her to her feet. Her lips brushed his cheek when she started away. "Wait," he called after her. "You have a rain slicker?"

"Yes," she said.

"Put it on," he told her just as he felt the first raindrops hit his face.

The others were awake now, pulling themselves together, and he found Denise dressed and staring up at the sky. "I've an extra rain slicker I can give you," he said. She hesitated. "Take it," he growled.

"All right." She shrugged. "You're a girl's best friend."

He ignored the tartness in the comment, took the brown slicker from his saddlebag, and tossed it to her. She caught it and put it on as she walked away.

Julie appeared in a black rain slicker with a black hood and he halted beside her. "Which way?" he asked. "Anything familiar to you up here?"

She pointed to two high crags in the distance. "Yes. I remember those two formations. They seemed like twins to me. We went past them."

"Then that's the way we go," Fargo said. He started to turn to his horse when the four men approached him. He cast a glance at Tom Colson who was standing nearby.

"We're pulling out," the one said. "Reiber hired us to ride with him. He's gone now and we don't like it here and we've no reason to stay on."

Fargo glanced at Colson, who shrugged. "Guess not," Fargo said to the four men. "You'll never make it down the way we came up."

"We sure know that. We'll ride north. There's got to be another way down someplace," the man said.

"Good luck to you," Fargo said. He received only answering nods as the men turned away.

The rain had begun to come down harder and Fargo signaled to the others to mount up. He led the way with Julie beside him and Denise riding near but apart from Colson and his men. They hadn't gone more than another hour when the rain began to come down heavily, the only blessing an absence of wind.

Fargo rode forward along the flat land between the hills and harsh rock formations, and he soon felt the ground beginning to grow soft under the Ovaro's hooves.

He kept tossing quick glances at Julie, but she seemed to be holding up well enough, her chin thrust forward determinedly. There was some toughness beneath that open and soft exterior, he saw.

The rain continued to come down hard and steady, and Fargo could see only a few feet ahead as he rode. But more disturbingly, the horse's feet were beginning to pull hard on the quickly softening ground. But he hadn't slipped or skidded yet, and Fargo decided to push on for as long as he could. He looked back at the others and saw the dim, rainswept figures, heads lowered, plodding after him. They had bunched together more, he took note—all except Denise, who continued to ride by herself.

With no sun or shadows to mark time, with only the grayness and the rain, Fargo could only guess at how long they rode through the downpour. The rain obscured any glimpse of the twin high crags, but at the slow pace they rode he knew there was little chance they'd reach them, much less go past. The rain poured in unrelenting steadiness and Fargo glanced up at the side of the stony hill they rode alongside. It rose up in a series of steplike ledges, he saw, and he had just taken his eyes away from the hill when the sound suddenly crashed over them.

"Shit," Fargo swore as the rushing, swooshing roar filled the air. He recognized it instantly for what it was. He whirled in the saddle as he yanked the Ovaro's head around sharply. "Up there, on those ledges," he shouted through the sound. "As high as you can go."

"What is it?" Julie asked as she spun her horse to follow him.

"Flash flood," he said. "The water's roaring down one of the high draws. It could turn down any of these passages. If it's this one and we're in it, your search is over." He spurred the Ovaro upward, bounded over one ledge and up to another, and his eyes searched the scrambling figures for Denise until he found her moving up the far end of the ledges.

"Get onto one of these steps and stay there," Fargo shouted at the top of his lungs as he felt the pinto slip and quickly regain its footing.

The roar had grown louder, a frightening sound. He halted with Julie on one of the stone steplike ridges and peered through the rain. The others were scattered atop the half-dozen steps when suddenly the water appeared, rushing down the passage where they had been. A brown, frothing, seething, bubbling mass of awesome speed and power, it swept through the empty passage, and Fargo heard Julie's murmur.

"My God, we'd have been just carried away," she said. "If you hadn't heard it and known what it was, we'd be all dead."

"Would have been doesn't count," Fargo said.

She leaned from her saddle to press her hand into his face for a brief moment. "It does with me," she said, and his gaze returned to the water rushing along below. It was still flowing fast, but it had already lost its early fury.

"It'll be stopping soon. The water in the high draw has emptied out now," he said, and drew a deep breath of relief. His eyes stayed on the water, watching the flow become slower, shallower, and finally turn to small surges that washed along the ground until it finally ended completely. His lips pulled back as he stared at the ground below. It would be difficult to ride the passage, he knew, the ground made into mud by the churning waters. Until they passed the spot where the floodwaters had hurtled downward, it would be dangerous and sticky but they had no choice. They couldn't stay on the rainswept steps like so many blackbirds on a rail.

Fargo carefully began to guide the Ovaro downward. When he reached the passage, he immediately felt the horse's hooves sink deep in the softened earth and he let the pinto slowly make his own way. The others began to file down and fall in behind him. Gratefully, Fargo breathed, they had only a short distance to go before they reached the draw where the flash floodwaters had raced down and into the passage.

When they went past the spot, the ground grew

firmer again at once, unsoaked by the raging rush of water. Fargo moved doggedly forward as the rain continued to drench the high land with a steady, unrelenting downpour. Once again Fargo felt the ground turning to slippery mud under the pinto. The grayness had also grown darker. There wasn't too much of the day left, he was certain, and headed upward to the hills on his right, shielding his face from the rain.

Among the stony hills and craggy formations he spotted a protrusion of rock, deep enough and long enough to offer shelter from the direct downpour. He motioned to the others to follow and guided the Ovaro along the hill until he reached the shelter. He swung from the saddle and landed on the hard, dry stone under the overhang. He shed his poncho and leaned it against the back wall to let the water drip from it as the others rode in under the overhead ledge. "We stay here for the night," he said, and watched Tom Colson dismount and go to Julie.

"You all right, Julie?" the man asked.

"I'm doing fine, Tom." She smiled and squeezed his arm reassuringly. Her face grew grave. "I hope it will be worth the terrible price we're paying. We have to keep believing, I guess."

"I guess," Colson said, and he moved away.

The grayness turned into night and the rain continued. Fargo sat down against the back wall of the overhang and listened to the rain beat onto the ledge overhead. Julie came and settled down next to him and only moments passed when Denise appeared and sank down wordlessly on the other side of him.

"Good night," she murmured.

" 'Night," Fargo said. He felt Julie's head turn to rest against his arm. When he looked down at her, she was asleep and he again marveled at her ability to sleep as quickly and easily as an infant could. He closed his eyes and went to sleep with the steady drum of the rain an ominous lullaby.

He slept heavily until the dry morning wind blew against his face and he opened his eyes. The sky remained gray but the rain had stopped. He rose quietly while Julie and Denise still slept, and walked out to survey the land.

The ordinarily brown earth was now a greenish-gray blanket of ominous silence. Fargo peered into the distance to where the twin crags rose up: they were still a distant goal. He turned away, the grimness held inside him, and used his canteen to wash as the others woke. He waited till they were finished pulling themselves together and gave them a moment to stare out across the land.

"It's stopped raining," Julie said happily. "And we can reach those twin crags in half a day's ride, I'd guess."

"Ordinarily, but there's an ocean of mud between us and those crags," Fargo said. "The rain has turned these hills into nothing but mud. Every surface, every piece of earth is mud, all of it waiting for something to set off a landslide of ooze."

"You saying we can't move on?" Colson asked.

"No, we have to move on," Fargo said with an eye to the sky. "It could rain more and make it even more dangerous."

"Hell, we can ride through mud," the man said.

"This mud is coating every hill, to the highest crags. It's just barely holding there. Too much vibration in any one spot could send it sliding down to bury everything below it," Fargo answered.

"What's too much vibration?" Julie asked.

"Any vibration that sends waves into one area enough to shake it loose. The vibration set off by the hooves of eight horses riding together could sure as hell do it. One horse could do it riding fast," Fargo said.

"What's the answer?" Tom Colson frowned.

"We ride singly, far apart, and on different levels. We'll be spaced so far apart that we'll hardly see one another until we reach the twin crags. That way the vibrations will be spread out evenly, nothing concentrated in any one area. If we do it right—and with a little luck—we can make it," Fargo said. His eyes scanned the others as they listened gravely. "I'll go down to the path below first. Two of you men will follow me," he said, nodding toward Colson's hands. "The first one will stay at least a hundred yards behind me at all times. The second rider stays a hundred yards behind him. Understand?" Both men nodded and Fargo turned to Colson. "You and your other two men will do the same, but you'll ride in the hills, across the middle," he said.

"All right." Colson nodded. "A hundred yards apart."

Fargo turned to Julie and Denise. "You two are the lightest so you'll ride the top of the hills. You'll stay riding the high land until we reach the two crags, Julie first, Denise a hundred yards behind. This way the vibrations will be spread out so they can be absorbed instead of setting off a mudslide."

"We keep our horses at a walk, I take it," Colson said.

"Everybody keeps to a walk," Fargo said. "And one thing more. If there is a slide, everybody stops and stays still. We don't want a panic that'll trigger maybe an ever bigger slide. Everybody understand?"

He received nods from all and motioned to Julie and Denise. "You two up to the high land first. Take it slow," he said. Julie nodded and waved at him. But Denise paused to exchange a grave glance with him. He nodded at her and she turned and followed Julie up the hill.

He watched them go, saw their horses slip a few

times but recover as they moved with deliberate slowness. When they reached the top of the hills, two small figures, they halted and Julie waved down at him.

Fargo sent Colson and two of his men out next, waited till they reached the middle high land in the hill, and then he climbed onto the Ovaro and began to move from the ledge to the low ground. He walked the horse forward, aware of the sliding softness of the earth. He glanced back when he'd gone some hundred yards to see the man behind him start to move from under the ledge.

Fargo nodded to himself in satisfaction and rode on. They all knew what they had to do. He could only hope they followed his instructions, and a grimace edged his lips. They were instructions, though, not assurances. Disaster could come of itself. A slide could happen at any time, triggered by its own conditions, the sheer weight of the mud or a loosening of the earth beneath the soft ooze. He could only hope for the best.

Once more he peered ahead to where the twin crags rose in the distance. It would be more than a half-day's ride at the slow pace they'd be traveling, he knew, and he listened to the sucking sound the pinto made every time he pulled a foot free of the mud.

As he rode, Fargo's eyes scanned the hills to his right, and from time to time he glanced back and glimpsed the man following him. He caught an occasional glimpse of Colson and the rider behind him in the middle of the hills, but Julie was out of sight on the high ground and Denise much too far back to see. His eyes swept the land again and he grimaced at the silence of it. The great gray-green expanse of muddied earth seemed an evil spirit lying in wait for its prey to make but one mistake that would unleash its fury. He rode on in uneasy silence.

But he knew, step by step, they were moving toward

the twin crags, which were now visibly closer. He peered toward the tall formations and grunted in satisfaction as he saw that the land surrounding them was flat. He came to a place where the hill to his right swept upward in a long, concave slope with but a few black-walnut trees in the center. At the top, a line of alders obscured Julie and Denise, but he saw Tom Colson start across the center of the long slope, the rider behind him not yet in sight.

Fargo brought his eyes back to the land ahead of him when the silence tore apart with sound, a primitive hissing, sucking noise. He spun in the saddle to stare up at the long, concave slope. The earth was moving, the greenish-gray mantle sliding downward with what seemed ridiculous slowness but he knew was not at all slow.

Colson looked up, horror flooding his face, tried to turn his horse away but it was a futile attempt. The horse slipped, almost fell, but it made little difference as the great wave of mud swept down onto Colson to engulf him in its suffocating embrace. As Fargo watched, the man and his horse disappeared inside the wave of mud.

The sucking sound continued until the slide reached the bottom of the slope. It halted there, piling up, on itself until it was a ten-foot mound of quivering earth.

Fargo's eyes went to the hillside and he saw the rider following Colson halted in the distance, frozen in place. The slide had left a narrow pathway of cleared hill to its left, and Fargo sent the Ovaro racing up the passage, the horse able to dig its hooves into ground that was soft but firm.

He reached the top, turned south, and crossed the high land to spot Julie, on the ground beside her horse. She had her face buried in her hands when he reached her and she was rocking back and forth. He leapt to the ground beside her, knelt down, and she pulled her face from her hands, her cheeks tearstained.

"My God, my God," she cried out as she clung to him. "I saw it through the trees from back there. It was horrible . . . horrible."

Fargo lifted her to her feet and she continued to cling to him, her compact body shaking. "You couldn't have helped him. No one could," he told her.

"I don't know, I don't know about any of it now," Julie half-sobbed.

He pressed his hands hard into her shoulders and straightened her up. "We can talk more later. Right now you've got to keep on till we reach those crags," he said sternly. "You stay up here. It's safest. That's why I put you and Denise up here."

Her round blue eyes stared up at him with almost childlike trust and obedience. "Whatever you say, Fargo," she murmured. "If you promise we can talk later."

"I promise," he said, and took his hands from her shoulders. He looked back and saw Denise halted in the distance. His eyes went down the hill to where the others were frozen in place with a combination of fear and uncertainty. He cupped his hands around his mouth as he called out. "We're going on. There's nothing we can do here," he said. "Keep your positions. Everything same as before."

He sent the Ovaro down the narrow pathway the mudslide had carved out, then he returned to his position at the bottom of the hills and moved forward once again. He fought down the impulse to quicken his pace. The hills on both sides were still waiting, ready to engulf anyone who made a mistake.

The sky had lightened, the threat of more rain gradually fading away, he noted with gratefulness, and he glanced up to the top of the hills. Both Julie and Denise were visible as the tree cover thinned, and he returned his gaze to the terrain ahead. The mud below the pinto's feet was beginning to dry out, and the two tall crags were coming into clear view. The land surrounding them was not as flat as it had seemed from far off, and he noticed many low hills with good tree growth. But he saw no harsh, steep slopes, and he grunted inwardly in satisfaction.

The long shadows streaked the land now. Another two hours till nightfall, he guessed. But they'd reach the twin crags first, and he permitted the pinto to increase his stride a little and stayed satisfied at the feel of the ground. The worst of it was behind them, the steep hills dropping off and the danger of killing mudslides vanishing.

The Trailsman slowed as he reached the twin crags, and he brought his horse to a halt alongside a half-circle of serviceberry that fronted one of the low hills. A bed of switchgrass stretched out from the trees and he let the Ovaro graze. He was leaning against a tree when the first of the two men behind him arrived, the second following soon.

They dismounted and sank to the ground, the strain visible on their faces, and in a little while the other two of Colson's men arrived. They were quick to sink to the ground also, and Fargo waited for Julie to arrive. When she did, he saw she looked surprisingly composed, but when she dismounted, she went to a corner, sat down, and rested her head against her drawn-up knees. He let her have her moment alone.

Denise arrived soon, dismounted, and drew a deep breath of relief. While two of the men gathered wood for a small fire, Fargo paused beside Denise as she sank back against a tree trunk. "Did you see any of it?" he asked. "Did Colson do anything to set it off, spur his horse faster, anything like that?"

"I was too far back to see it," she answered. "And it was over when I came in sight of it. I saw Julie first, then the mud sliding down to the bottom." She drew another deep sigh. "I'm damn glad it's over," she breathed. Her eyes went to where Julie still sat with her head down. "She'll be wanting comforting again tonight, of course," Denise slid out.

"Something wrong with that, dammit?" Fargo snapped, angry at her tone. "I'd say that was pretty normal."

"So long as it's not too much comforting," Denise sniffed.

"I heard that before," he muttered, and strode away from her, still angry at the streak of possessiveness that persisted in her. Unwarranted and unwelcome, he grunted. She'd no right to it. But that wouldn't bother Denise, he knew, and he pushed aside further thoughts as he sank down beside Julie. She lifted her hand and, dry-eyed, peered at him.

"There's some beef jerky left to warm over the fire. Have some. You have to eat something," he told her, and she nodded.

"When can we talk?" she asked.

"Later, when everyone's asleep. I'll bed down up on that low hill just behind us," he said, and she nodded obediently.

She ate some of the warmed beef jerky when dark came and the simple meal was taken in almost total silence. When it ended, Denise took her blanket off by herself and the four men stretched out together, everyone plainly feeling the need of a long night's sleep. Julie sat alone, head bowed.

Fargo took his bedroll and walked up the hill until he could no longer see the campsite. He set his things down beneath the low-branched serviceberry and un-dressed to his Levi's, the holster and Colt by his side. The night grew deep, and though he couldn't see the camp below, he heard the sounds of snoring and rest-less turnings.

Another sound came to his ears, someone moving up the hill with uncertain steps. "Over here," he called softly, and saw her figure materialize through the trees, the loose pajamas swaying as she moved. She sank down beside him, her round-cheeked face grave.

"Maybe we shouldn't go on," Julie said. "Maybe it's been a message, a sign."

"What do you want to do?" Fargo asked.

"That depends."

"On what?"

"On how much you'll help me," she said, and Fargo felt the stab of surprise at her words. She leaned closer and the high, round breasts pressed against the pajama top. "I've done a lot of thinking. I've thought about what Tom and Uncle Cyrus would want me to do. They'd want me to go on. They wanted to help me find my daddy's will and the map. I owe it to them to go on. I owe it to them not to make their terrible deaths senseless and meaningless. Can you understand that, Fargo?"

"I suppose so," Fargo said, unwilling to tell her how much she might be misjudging her uncle and her stepfather.

Her hands pressed against his chest; her eyes peered into his with soft pleading. "But I can't go on alone. I need you to help me," she said. "I need your strength. You've become part of this, Fargo. Finish it with me."

"I'll do whatever I can, Julie," he said, her pleading reaching out to him, the combination of sweetness and determination, helpless little girl and warm, needing woman, impossible to turn down.

Her arms encircled his neck and Julie's mouth pressed his, sweet softness that quickly turned hungering. Her lips worked over his, pressed, pulled, sucked. "Oh, Fargo . . . mmmmm, oh, mmmmmm," she murmured. "I can't help it. I need you. I need to forget." Her hands moved across his naked chest, pressed, caressed, came to his Levi's, her fingers pushed beneath the waistband, retreated, fumbled again. He reached down and unbuttoned the trousers, and her hands pressed against his muscled abdomen and she gasped. Her exploding, almost frantic wanting surprised him as he slid the Levi's off and her mouth returned to his, her tongue suddenly darting forward, circling inside his lips. Her hands pressed against his face, moved down across his neck and shoulders, flattened hard against his chest.

"Fargo," she breathed, her eyes half-closed and the pale-yellow hair falling half over his face. Suddenly the little girl had become a devouring, wanting woman, yet her sweet face remained at odds with her sensuous wanting. He was still taken aback, he realized, still wrestling with surprise when she drew back and her hands flew to the tops of the pajamas, pulling open the buttons with fury. She flung the top away and let him admire the very round, high breasts, almost complete circles of creamy white, each tipped by a flat little nipple of delicate pink on a circle only a shade darker.

Julie waited, letting Fargo gaze at her with obvious pride and pleasure. Then she came forward to him and he reached out to cup the round mounds in both hands. "Aaaaah," she gasped, and her mouth was on his again, pulling, sucking, opening wide to cover his lips entirely. Suddenly she pulled back, rose to her knees, and yanked at the drawstring of the loose pajama trousers. They fell away to reveal a slightly convex little belly under a short waist and, below it, a curly tangle of light-tan hair that extended beyond the V to send little blondish trails along her inner thighs.

Her legs were not long but young and firm and quivering with vitality; she had round knees and short, muscular calves and he admired the compact, energy-filled sensuality of her body. Julie flung herself against him and gasped in pleasure at the touch of skin upon skin, the warmth of tactile enjoyment, and he turned with her, swung her onto her back as his burgeoning, eager maleness came against the blondish nap.

"Aaaah, oh, yes . . . mmmmmm," Julie gasped, and he brought his mouth to one creamy white, round breast, pulled gently, then harder, and she cried out again. His tongue circled the tiny, flat nipple, slid across it and back again, and he felt it quiver but hardly rise. Julie's hands came to his neck, pressed his head harder against her breast.

"Mmmmmm, mmmmm," Julie moaned. "More, more, oh, God, yes." Her head moved from side to side suddenly as she cried out in pleasure while his hand traced a slow, insinuating path along the bottom of her breasts, pressed the softness of each, then moved down across her rib cage and the small waist.

Her mouth worked feverishly under his once more as his hand paused at her tiny belly button, exploring, circling, and then closed over the small, convex belly. "Oh, oh, aaaaaaah," Julie breathed as he caressed the slight bulge, pressing his hand harder against it before he moved his palm down to the light-tan V. His fingers pushed through the curly tangle, pressuring the small pubic mound beneath, and reached down between her thighs. "Ah, ah, aaaah," Julie breathed as his fingers touched the moist lips, tantilizing the maddeningly sensitive little lip of flesh, and Julie screamed in absolute delight.

Her short, compact thighs fell open and her hands clutched at his buttocks, pulling at him, trying to bring him atop her. He obeyed, his swollen organ seeking the eternal warmth of that special haven. He came to her open, quivering lips and pushed partly in. Julie screamed out in protest. "No, no . . . all the way, oh, God, please Fargo, please." Her round blue eyes stared at him with something close to despair and the Cupid's-bow mouth worked feverishly as her lips made little sounds of wanting. He pushed in deeper and Julie wailed, lifting her hips and thrusting upward to enclose all of him. When he thrust forward completely to push against the soft walls, she pulled his face down onto the very round breasts, pushed them against his mouth.

Her softly fleshed, compact thighs opened and closed around him as Julie began to pump upward with his every thrust. "Yes, yes, mmmmmm, oh, yes, oh, my God," she gasped out. "I want you, Fargo, I want you." Her head tossed from side to side, the pale-yellow hair a cascade of light in the night. The sweet, almost innocent goodness had been transformed into a wildly devouring package of high-energy sensuousness.

The surprise still ate at Fargo along with the delicious warmth of her around his organ. He felt himself quickening, her absolute wanting fanning the fires of his senses beyond control. But she suddenly half-screamed, a cry cut off in midair and followed by a rush of harsh breath and small, gasped breaths as she drew her round little belly in and out. Her hands clasped against his buttocks as she lifted her torso up, hung in midair as the harsh gasps erupted in a wailing scream.

"Oh, oh, aaaaiiiiieeeee . . . aaaiiiieeee," Julie screamed as the world exploded for her. He felt his own ecstasy, pulsating against her moist softness, flesh absorbing flesh, sensation encompassing itself as his face lay against the high round breasts, one flat tip in his mouth when the moment of eternity made mortal vanished. Julie's scream collapsed into a despairing cry and her compact, warm body finally fell back onto his bedroll, the round breasts rising and falling deliciously with her every long, deep breath. When she finally breathed easily again, she stared at him as he lay half over her warm, compact loveliness, and suddenly all the little-girl sweetness flooded into her round-cheeked face again, her eyes wide with trusting openness.

"You're full of surprises," he remarked.

She blinked at him with seriousness as her arms

encircled his neck. "I surprised myself, too," she murmured. "I didn't know needing and wanting were so much the same thing." She pulled his head down to rest against her breasts for a moment and then pushed him back and frowned into his eyes. "Are you disappointed in me?" she questioned gravely, all little girl again.

"No, no," he said quickly. "Hell, I'll take that kind of surprise anytime."

"I had to shut out the past and open tomorrow."

He nodded. It was as good an explanation as any. "You did a good job of it," he told her, and Julie smiled, a warm, contented smile, then turned and cradled herself against him, her round, firm breasts pressed into his chest, pale-yellow hair lying against his shoulder.

"Good night," she murmured, and he watched her fall asleep almost at once. Again, he marveled at her ability to shake away the world. Unwilling to wonder about what was perhaps beyond answering, he closed his eyes and pulled sleep around himself.

9

Morning came with a bright sun and Julie woke with Fargo. He was sad to see her lovely compact shape disappear into the pajamas.

"I'll see you below. I want to get back before the others wake," she said.

"I'd guess they're still asleep. It was a hard day," Fargo said, and she blew him a kiss as she hurried away. He rose, took his time gathering up his bedroll, and walked down the hillside to the camp. Julie was behind a tree changing when he reached the camp and the others were just waking. All except Denise, he saw. She was dressed and beside her horse. When he arrived, she turned, waited while he used his canteen to freshen up, and then she came toward him, her walk deliberately slow, longish breasts swaying in unison under her shirt. A cool smile almost masked the flame in her beige eyes. She halted and the smile suddenly disappeared.

"Bastard," she hissed. "You did it, damn you."

"Do what?" he asked with hasty innocence.

"Little Miss Goodness, that's what," Denise hissed again, growing fury in her voice. "I'm really surprised."

"Surprised at what? What are you talking about?"

"That Little Miss Goodness screws and that you screwed her. Damn you!"

"Now, you're just jumping to conclusions."

"Hell I am. I woke last night and decided to find

you. I went halfway up the hillside. I didn't have to go any farther," Denise said. Suddenly there was hurt in her voice, not just anger.

Fargo swore inwardly. "I didn't plan it, didn't expect it. One thing led to another," he said.

"Doesn't it always?" she snapped tartly, and her eyes blazed at him as a half-sneer touched her red lips. "Tell me one thing: did she say oh-golly-gee when she came?" she speared.

He felt his lips tighten. "No she didn't, and that's none of your damn business," he growled. "You're just plain, old-fashioned jealous."

"Of her?" Denise shot back. "Never. I just expected you were the kind who'd want your pussy to be a mountain lion not a kitty cat."

Fargo felt his irritation with her grow. "Let's say she was a surprise," he said, unwilling to be more specific yet wanting to sting her enough to shut her down. It seemed to work.

Denise's eyes narrowed and she fastened him with a suddenly thoughtful, long glance. "No kidding?" she said with thoughts still racing behind the beige eyes.

"No kidding," he said coldly.

Her lips pursed in thought for a moment and then she turned on her heel without another word and strode away. She went to her horse and began to mount up when he crossed to her in three long strides.

"Where are you going?" He frowned.

"Away from here," she said icily.

"Without your money?" he jabbed.

She didn't lose her cool composure as her eyes met his. "I decided there are too many ways to be short-changed around here," she said.

His hand caught her by the arm. "You can't make it all the way back alone, dammit."

"I'll make it. I'm a hard-nose, remember?" she tossed back.

"That's not being a hard-nose. That's being stupid," he snapped.

"Don't you worry about little me."

He let a long sigh escape him. "Look, think it through tonight, at least," he asked, hoping to buy time for her to simmer down. "Let's talk more about all this before you go running off and get yourself killed, scalped, or whatever."

"I'll think about it," she said, her face set. It was as much as he could hope for now, he realized, and he squeezed her arm as he turned away.

"Mount up," he tossed back to her, and saw the others were ready to ride. He crossed to the pinto.

Julie was waiting on her horse. "I didn't realize she was that fond of you," she said, and there was only a hint of sadness in her voice.

"Denise is quick to assume things," he said. "Which way, now? You remember anything more?"

"Yes, we went past these two crags for a spell. There was a high quarry on a broad hill, four abandoned mines on it. There was something about one of them. I'm sure it'll come to me when we get there," she said.

"Good. Let's ride," Fargo said, and set out with Julie beside him. Denise came along a dozen yards back, he saw, Colson's four men riding together behind her.

The ground had almost completely dried out. Perhaps this region had never received the full downpour, he mused.

Low rocky hills bordered their path and the sun had reached the noon sky when he found a highland pond, spring-fed, large enough to fill their canteens with fresh, cold water and let the horses drink their fill.

Julie's little smiles carried an extra measure of meaning and she seemed quietly content. She could indeed put away the past, he reflected.

"Mount up," he called out when everyone had cooled off enough, and started to climb onto the Ovaro when one of the men called out.

"Not us, Fargo," the man said, and Fargo brought his leg down and faced the four men. "We feel the way Cy Reiber's boys did. Colson's gone. He paid us to ride with him. We've no reason to stay on, 'less you want to hire us on yourself," the man said.

Fargo shot a glance at Julie.

"I see no reason for that," she said to the men. "Though you're welcome to stay."

"No, thanks," the man said. "We'll be going back then." He turned away and the others followed him to their horses.

Fargo watched them ride off in silence, not that there was anything to say, and his glance went to Denise. She was on her horse, her face coldly impassive. He climbed onto the pinto and she fell back a dozen yards as he rode on with Julie beside him.

The trail suddenly grew steeper, became a series of low mounds they had to climb up and down until it suddenly flattened out again. He glanced back and saw Denise quietly following, staying at least a dozen yards behind. The trail grew steep again and led up and down once more, with another series of low mounds that were bordered by granite rock formations. This high country was still iron-ore land, he noted, though the old miners must have had a hell of a time getting the stuff down from here, he reflected.

The rock-bordered mounds continued on the passage and he quickened the pace to get past their undulating dips and inclines. Finally, the trail flattened out once more and he halted and looked back for Julie to come into sight. He waited and a frown began to creep over his brow. He continued to stare back along the trail as he waited for Denise to come along.

"Damn," he swore suddenly when she failed to

appear at all. "Stay here," he told Julie, and sent the Ovaro racing back along the trail. His eyes on the ground, he raced the horse over the hilly trail and knew what had happened. She had waited till she was low in one of the dips and taken off. He galloped on until he skidded the horse to a halt where a set of hoofprints appeared, a lone horse. They turned into a tall rock formation that climbed up along a hill and he saw three narrow passages fanning out through the rocks.

Each was a solid stone path, he cursed, and he'd no way of knowing which she had taken. There'd be no prints to follow in any of them. She had picked the right place and the right moment to cut out, damn her. To chase up the passages in the rocks would be an exercise in futility. They undoubtedly fanned out into still other passages as they climbed up into the rocks. She had taken a page out of his own book. His lips a grim line, he backed the Ovaro around and rode on along the trail again until he reached Julie.

Her round blue eyes questioned. "She cut out," he muttered. "Took off on her own. She said she'd think it out through the night, damn her."

"She probably decided there was nothing more to think about," Julie said. "She probably decided she could still catch up to Tom's men."

"No, that's not her style. She'll try to go it alone," Fargo said, and spurred the horse forward. "Let's move." Maybe Denise would have an attack of common sense and return, he told himself with more hope than conviction. He surprised himself at being as bothered as he was, he realized. She had her own hard-nosed appeal, partly made of uncompromising cynicism that she'd nonetheless kept from sliding into bitterness. And for all her goodness and little-girl sweetness, Julie was less the lost one than Denise, he decided.

"Things happen because they're supposed to happen, Fargo," Julie said, cutting into his thoughts. Her words and her tone had a calmness that he unexplainably found irritating.

"People make things happen, by what they do and what they don't do," he said, and was sorry for his own curtness.

But Julie only smiled with sweet understanding. "Maybe it's some of both," she said. "You cared for her, didn't you?"

"I felt sorry for her," Fargo answered, the reply not entirely untrue, and Julie's hand reached out and pressed his arm.

"I'll see that you don't think too much about her." She smiled and he allowed a laugh of acceptance.

They were into midafternoon when Fargo reined up as the wide, broad hillside appeared in front of them, dotted with alders and shadbush and the trails of abandoned mine diggings. Four abandoned mines, he counted, their entrances boarded with loosely nailed lengths of pinewood.

"Yes, this is the place," Julie breathed. "There, that one on the right, two trees growing on each side of the entrance. It's all coming back to me now, Fargo." She slapped her horse on the rump and sent the animal bounding up the hillside along one of the old mining-cart trails.

He followed and caught up to her as she halted and jumped to the ground outside the entranceway to the old mine.

"It's inside. Everything's inside, the map and the will. He put it in a tin box. I remember it all now," she said, and went to the slats of wood that covered the entrance. She began to tear at them, and one came off easily, rotted with age and weather.

Fargo pulled at the others and they came off with equal ease until the mine shaft entrance rose before them, the remains of an old mine cart just inside.

"Let's go in," Julie said, excitement in her voice.

"Not so fast," he said. "These old mines build up gases and air so foul it can kill. Let some of the fresh air in first and some of what's inside out." He took her arm and drew her to one side of the entranceway, leaned against a rock until close to an hour had passed. "Let's give it a try now," he said, and Julie was close at his side as he walked into the mine shaft. The dank, musty odor assailed his nostrils at once when he went a dozen feet down the shaft. Old, partly rusted pick-axes and shovels lined one earthen wall, and it was Julie who first spotted the hurricane lamp on the ground.

She knelt beside it. "There's kerosene in it, a lot of it. Let's see if it works," she said, and he handed her a match. She rested it against the kerosene spout and, to Fargo's surprise, the lamp lighted at once. Julie turned the lamp up and its yellow light flooded the low mine shaft. She handed the lamp to him. "You take it," she said, and picked up one of the old short-handled mining shovels. She pointed to a circular row of stones that surrounded a fairly deep drill shaft, large enough for two men to work in.

Fargo raised the lamp over the shaft, leaned forward, and drew back as the odor rose up from the bottom, heavy and dank yet acrid and sharp. Drawing a deep breath, he held the lamp over the shaft again and peered down. The bottom seemed filled with stale water that undoubtedly covered years of sediment, soil, and small rocks, all contributing to create the gaseous odor that drifted upward as the air from outside trailed into the mine.

Fargo glanced at Julie.

She stood near him, the shovel in her hand. "Did you see anything down there that looked like a tin box?" she asked.

"No, but then it could be buried under the water and silt. Is that where he put it?" Fargo asked.

"I can't remember for sure, either in there or in the next drill hole. Look again, Fargo, please," she said, and he turned to the deep, round hole again, lifted the kerosene lamp high, and let it illuminate as much of the shaft as it could. He saw nothing that looked like a tin box, not on the surface of the silt and water. He had just drawn back and started to turn when the blow smashed into the side of his head. He felt the lamp drop from his hand as he staggered, his head pounding and a gray curtain over his eyes.

"Julie . . ." he heard himself manage to call out as the gray curtain grew heavier. He fell to one knee, tried to shake his head, and something slammed into his chest. He felt himself going backward, falling, sensations pushing through the gray curtain, the rush of air past his face, falling downward, his arm hitting against something, and then he lost consciousness almost entirely. The world grew still, became almost a void, yet he clung to a vestige of awareness, fought against the gray curtain, and managed to shake his head. Sensation again, wetness, against his hand. The gray curtain began to lift a fraction and his nostrils drew in sharp, acrid air; he felt himself cough. The motion sent a wave of pain through his head while it tore the gray curtain aside. He blinked, shook his head, and the remainder of the curtain vanished.

He felt the water around his legs and something more, the heavy touch of wet soil and sediment, and again the very strong, heavy odor assailed his nostrils, almost suffocating. He looked upward, stared at the circular walls of earth that surrounded him, and realization pushed its way into his now fully conscious mind. He was at the bottom of the drill shaft, in the water and sediment and gases that lay at the very bottom. He peered up into the blackness above. Had a piece of shoring given way and come down on him? Had it smashed into Julie, too?

"Julie," he shouted. He pushed with both hands and managed to stand up in the silt and water. "Julie," he shouted again. "Down here." He waited and heard nothing. "Julie, can you hear me?" He shouted at the top of his lungs, then had to stop and cough as he drew in a mouthful of the fetid air.

He stopped his coughing and stared up the round shaft, straining his ears, and suddenly he heard something, a faint, scraping sound. Excitement and hope leapt inside him. "Julie? Are you up there?" he shouted again, and listened. "Julie, down here," he screamed, and then, as he peered up along the drill hole, he saw the flicker of light intrude on the blackness at the top. It grew brighter and then he saw the kerosene lamp held over the top of the shaft and Julie's face beside it, pale-yellow hair bright in the lamplight. "Good God, you're all right," Fargo said.

"Quite all right," Julie said. "A lot more than you are, my dear."

Fargo stared up and a frown slid across his brow. He wondered if he had heard garbled words, strange echoes down the long shaft. "Look around up there, Julie. There's probably some old rope. What happened?" he called up.

"What happened?" Julie echoed in a tone of calm sweetness that dug the furrow deeper into his brow. "I hit you with the shovel. I thought you'd just go over the edge, but I had to hit you again."

Fargo heard her words spiral down the shaft to him, heard them circle through his mind and could find only a massive sense of disbelief inside himself. Perhaps he was still unconscious, he wondered, or having some kind of nightmare. He blinked, shook his head, and stared up to the top of the shaft again.

Julie was still there, still holding the light so she could see. And she was smiling, a tolerant, almost pitying smile. "You did become an unexpected problem," she said. "But it worked out quite well. Nobody will ever hear from you again. You'll just vanish and maybe in a hundred years, if anyone ever does look in these old mines, they'll find your bones. Maybe."

Fargo felt the frown digging so deep into his brow that it hurt as he stared up at the pale-yellow hair and the round-cheeked face under it. "Why?" he called out, and knew he sounded not only confounded but plaintive. "Why?"

"You got in the way. You came into it and then I had to bring you along until I found the right time and place," she said. "It was only going to be Cyrus and Tom Colson at first."

"You killed them?" Fargo blurted, another wave of astonishment sweeping through him.

"Cyrus was easy. I was behind him on that terrible ledge. I just hit his horse on the rump with my reins. He reared and fell," she said almost airily in her tinkly voice. "Tom Colson was only a little more difficult. I had to plan it right, but you spelled out the way for me, the vibrations that would cause a slide." Fargo heard the groan escape his lips. "When Denise was too far back to see, I made my horse buck and jump right over where Tom rode below. It worked just the way you said it would."

Fargo's stare still held only incredulity, and the single question came from his lips again. "Why?" he asked.

"Daddy's will gave them each a quarter of the silver," she said. "He told me he was leaving it to Uncle Cy for taking care of me if that came to be and keeping tabs on everything if it didn't. He couldn't know Tom Colson would come along to marry Mother, but he provided another quarter of the silver for anyone who did just that."

"And you had to kill them for that?" Fargo frowned.

"They didn't deserve any of it. Cyrus was just a

greedy old man. That's the only reason he kept in contact with me, so he could claim his share when the time came. And Tom Colson knew he was in for a quarter. Daddy had told Mother about the will and she'd told him. That's the only reason he stuck around."

Fargo felt the astonishment dropping away from him, the gargantuan disbelief falling aside finally and in its place another kind of amazement, this one made of fury and icy contempt. "You little bitch," he said. "You two-faced, scheming, rotten little bitch. All that goodness and love and caring, it was all just a damn mask, an act."

"It was necessary. I had to wait all these years for the time to come, so I polished my role."

"Then you never needed either of them to help you remember the right place," Fargo said.

"That's right. I knew just where it was. The box with the will and the map was hidden behind one of the stones around the top of this shaft. I just took it out. But I did need them to get me here. I couldn't have reached here alone. Too many Indians, too many things to stop me from making it. When I realized how much they were set on battling each other, I just let things take their course, knowing that one or the other would get me here."

"Then I showed up to give you extra insurance," Fargo said bitterly.

"Yes, wasn't that nice?" Julie said, and her tinkly laugh drifted down the mine shaft.

The thought stabbed through Fargo's mind, all the truth of it suddenly hitting at him. Denise had been right about her from the very start. Not the words, just the music, and he swore silently at himself.

Julie's voice broke into his dark thoughts. "It's all over now. I'll tear up the will, even though neither Uncle Cyrus nor Tom is around to lay claim, and I've the map that tells me where the silver is hidden. Not far from here, from what I can see, in one of the other mines."

He saw her step back and take the lamp with her and the darkness flooded down from the top of the shaft. "No, goddamn you," he shouted. "You can't leave me here."

Her voice drifted down from above, the tinkly, airy sound of it unchanged. "But I am. You're a dead man, Fargo. It'll take a little longer than it did with Cyrus and Tom, but the end will be the same." He heard her pause for a moment and then her voice came again. "Look at the bright side, Fargo. You had the pleasure of screwing me, and it was good. None of the others had that." He heard her tinkly laugh as the sound of her footsteps faded away.

"No, damn you. Come back," he shouted, more out of desperation and fury than anything else. She wouldn't come back. He knew that, yet he continued to send curses after her until he finally stopped and peered upward. The shaft was almost pitch-black, but a faint glimmer of light found its way into the mine from the opened entranceway. It was hardly anything, yet it was enough to let him still see the round walls of the shaft. Even that would end when day fled, he knew, and he moved with desperation, splashing the stale, dirty water as he ran his fingers along the earth walls. Somehow he had to climb out of the shaft, he knew, or Julie's words would come all too true. No one would enter the abandoned old mine for countless years. He would die of starvation in time, he realized. But he'd probably die first of the acrid, dank gas that rose up from the silt and sediment at the bottom of the shaft. Given but a little time, it would fill his lungs, saturate the bottom of the shaft, and he'd have no way of escaping from its killing penetration.

Days, Fargo bit out silently, perhaps a week of growing weaker and weaker until he'd be helpless, no more able to escape the shaft than the water and sediment. He continued to run his fingers along the circular walls of the shaft. The earth was bumpy yet slippery, coated with untold years of accretions formed by gas, water that seeped its way into the mine, and earth organisms that formed a slime over every bit of the shaft walls.

Fargo tried to dig his fingers into the earth walls and found his hands slip and slide. He tried to use his heels, with the same results. With careful deliberation, he went around the walls again, feeling his way along every inch only to end with a curse of frustration. There was no break, no ridge, no bulge that would afford a place to start climbing, and as he leaned back, he felt himself shake as a cough racked his body.

The cough persisted, but he finally brought it under control and slumped down in the water and silt. He felt the weakness come over him and knew it was the gas that made him feel nauseated. The last dim trickle of daylight left the mine entrance and the drill hole became utterly and totally black, so black he couldn't see his hands. He knew he had to inhale as little of the gas as possible, and he leaned back against the earth wall and forced himself to take shallow breaths. Finally, sleep came to him despite his efforts to fight it away, and he sat with his body bunched up against the round wall in a sleep of exhaustion until he woke.

He blinked his eyes in the blackness and had no idea how much time had passed. The blackness made his world a void where space and time ceased to exist. But little by little, the terribly faint light drifted to the top of the shaft again and he knew it was day outside.

He pushed himself to his feet, shook away a wave of weakness, and forced himself to concentrate on finding a way to scale the unscalable, slime-covered shaft. Suddenly he laughed, threw his head back and laughed again. He dropped to one knee and drew the thin, double-edged throwing knife from his calf holster. With excitement pulling at him, he began to dig into the earth wall of the shaft. When he passed the outer layer, the earth grew stiffer and he had to work carefully or risk breaking the blade. But he kept on, fighting off waves of weakness and nausea as the noxious air flowed around him. When he pulled back and ran his fingers over the wall, he had carved three toeholds in the earth, and he faced the wave of despair that swept over him.

Three toeholds, and he had taken perhaps all day. He had no way of knowing, but he felt the weakness flooding through his body. He lowered himself into the stale water and rested again, his back against the round wall. When strength returned to him, he rose and began to hack away at the wall again. The pattern became his existence, the very fiber of life itself, but carving each toehold grew almost impossibly difficult as he had to cling to the narrow places he had hacked out while reaching up to carve more. But fighting off the weakness that came again and then the cough that racked his body, he climbed up on the places he had carved, pressed himself tight against the earth wall, and began to hack another foothold for himself.

Again, it was painful and slow, every muscle used to cling to the wall and yet reach his arm up far above his head. He shook away the tiny pieces of earth that fell on his face as he dug the knife into the wall, and he had paused to rest his burning shoulder and arm muscles when a wave of the acrid gas burst from the very bottom of the shaft. It flared up, swept over him, and he felt dizziness pull at him at once. His hand grasped for one of the places he had managed to carve in the wall, but his feet slipped and he fell back from his precarious perch. He tried to twist, but his body failed to respond and he slammed into the hard, circular wall of the shaft with his head.

A flash of yellow and orange burst inside his head and he toppled downward, felt the water with only the dimmest sense of recognition. He lay crumpled in the silt, the gas fumes engulfing him, an invisible, suffocating blanket. His head fell back, rested half in the stale, sediment-filled water. As he lay helpless, he was aware, in the strange and mysterious ways of existence, that the wings of death hovered over him in the blackness, and then the last glimmer of consciousness swept from him. The black silence wrapped itself around him, a shroud beyond his knowing.

10

Sensations. Softness. Warmth. His face touched. Death was not made of sensations. Thoughts. Questions. The mind alive. This was not death. Fargo lay unmoving as the thoughts built inside him, grew stronger. His eyelids moved and the thoughts became hope. It seemed a tremendous effort, but he pulled his eyelids open. Shapes. Colors. Unfocused blurs registered in front of him, and he blinked hard, then again and again. The unfocused patterns began to take on definition, grow clearer, finally find edges, shapes, details.

He heard the hoarse words rise from his throat. "My God," he managed. Gossamer brown hair, a short nose, beige eyes took shape in front of him. "Denise," he said, his voice a hoarse whisper.

"In person," he heard her say. "And you're alive, thank God." She blew a deep sigh from her lips, her cheeks puffing out. "I wasn't sure you'd make it."

Fargo lay still and the pictures came, flashed through his mind—himself at the bottom of the shaft, the terrible gases rising up, the fall as he tried to hack his way out—and just as suddenly the pictures fell away and his eyes focused on Denise again. He could see foliage, tree branches, a patch of blue. "Where am I?" he asked.

"Beside a pond."

Fargo managed to rise up on one elbow, fought off the wave of dizziness that swept over him, and the frown furrowed his brow as he looked down at himself. He was naked except for a small towel partly over his groin.

"Your clothes were filthy and saturated with the smell of the gases. I washed them and let them dry out in the sun," Denise said.

"How long?" Fargo asked, letting the question hang unfinished.

"This is the third day," she told him. "Most of the time I was sure you wouldn't make it. You were hardly breathing."

He felt strength begin to slowly flow back through his body, his muscles responding with tiny twitches. "How did you know?" he asked.

"I didn't."

"But you came back."

"Yes, but I didn't expect I'd find you at the bottom of a mine shaft," Denise said. "All I knew was the more I thought about Julie, the more certain I was that she was a damn fraud. I didn't keep on through the rocks. I pulled up, waited, wrestled some more with myself, and then came down and followed your tracks. I reached the hill with the four abandoned mines, and I'd just started up when I saw Julie come out of one. I ducked into some alders and watched her take her horse and ride across the hill to another of the old mine entrances. She tore off the boards and went in." Denise paused, peered hard at him. "Want some water?" she asked, and he nodded.

"Yes, that'd be good," he murmured, and she helped him sit up, put her canteen to his lips, and he drew in small sips first, then longer ones. The water was wonderfully cool and he felt his body refreshed at once. He sat back on his elbows when she put the canteen away.

"I didn't know what was going on. All I saw was Julie, so I stayed in the trees and waited. She came out of the mine with two sacks, made three more trips till she had eight sacks.''

"The silver," Fargo said.

"She put them on her horse, tied them to the horn, and rode slowly away. I still hadn't seen you," Denise said. "For all I knew, she was going to meet you someplace. I gave her plenty of distance and began to follow her. She rode till it grew dark, then she settled down for the night. When you were still no place around, I had a chilling fear and hoped I was wrong."

Denise paused, took a deep breath, and went on with her story. "I backed away from Julie and started back to the old mine I'd seen her leave. But it wasn't easy in the dark. She'd traveled a good way and I got lost a half-dozen times. Finally, I had to rest some myself."

"But you found me again," Fargo said. "Lucky for me."

"Not until morning and I could trace my way back again. When I finally reached the old mine, I went in and called and got no answer. I called a half-dozen times with no answer. I wondered if maybe you'd decided to cut out and leave her, but I knew that wouldn't be your style. Then I thought maybe you were lying hurt somewhere along the trail. I started to turn to look for you when you groaned. I hardly heard it, but I did," Denise said.

"Thank God for that," Fargo said.

"I saw the kerosene lamp by the wall near the mouth of the mine and turned it up. I moved deeper inside the mine and saw the drill shaft, lifted the light over the top of it, and saw you there at the bottom." Denise paused and her eyes narrowed at him. "I guessed you didn't fall in by accident," she said.

"You guessed right. She cracked me on the head with a shovel and then knocked me into the shaft."

"I was right about her all along, but I never thought she'd go that far," Denise muttered.

"She told me how she did in Reiber and Colson, too. Neither was an accident."

A low whistle of amazement escaped Denise's lips. "I never figured that of her."

"But you never bought her love-and-goodness routine. You knew something was wrong. She's not real, you said. How'd you stay so sure?" Fargo said.

Denise allowed a slow smile. "A woman can usually fool a man. She can seldom fool another woman," she said. "But she was good. I wasn't sure, not until . . ."

"Not until what?" Fargo frowned.

A wry edge came into her smile. "Until you told me she'd been a real surprise in your bedroll," Denise answered, and drew a questioning frown from him. "If Little Miss Goodness had been for real she wouldn't have been in your bedroll, and even if she were, she wouldn't have been a surprise. Sweet and sticky maybe, but no surprise," Denise finished with a trace of smugness.

Fargo stretched his body. Strength continued to return, he felt, and he peered at Denise with admiration. "One thing more," he said. "How in hell did you ever get me out of there?"

"I found some rope, old, heavy rope, and a pulley. I tied one end of the rope to a strong beam shoring up the ceiling. I brought it around the beam and used the pulley to form a makeshift block and tackle. I lowered myself down the shaft, tied the other end around you, climbed back to the top, and began to hoist you up using the rope. It was hard, even with the balance and leverage of the rope I'd rigged. But I finally got you to the top. I even brought up your throwing knife. The really hard part was getting you onto your horse so's we could get away from there."

"This time I owe you one," Fargo said.

"This makes us even," Denise said, and he sat up straight.

"Where are my clothes?" he asked.

"I'll get them for you," she said and disappeared past a half-circle of bushes to return with his things. She watched him dress, flex his muscles, and pull himself together. "What now?" she asked.

"I'm going after her," Fargo said. "She killed two men and damn near made me number three. She's not just a little two-faced liar. She's a murderess."

"Are you strong enough to ride?" Denise asked.

"I'll ride," he said grimly. "By tonight, I'll be my old self." He began to dress and flung aside the small waves of dizziness that continued to pull at him. But they were growing weaker and shorter, he noted, and he climbed onto the Ovaro with ease. "I'll drop you off someplace first," he said.

"I'm going with you. Might as well get my money in silver," Denise said.

He considered a moment. Little Julie Hudson had shown she could be deadly. "Same rules," he grunted. "We do things my way."

"All right," she said. "Hard-nose."

"That's my line," he said.

She rode down the hillside beside him. He had her show him where she'd followed Julie and then halted to ride back. He picked up Julie's horse's prints on the other side of where she had bedded down for the night, and he followed for another half-hour before the night descended. He halted under the wide branches of a hackberry and felt more exhausted than he wanted to feel. He quickly set out his bedroll and undressed and saw Denise spread her blanket a few feet from him.

"You going to stay there?" he asked.

"Definitely," she said.

"You going to be plain jealous again and hold a grudge?" he questioned.

"I'm not interested anymore," she said stiffly.

"Liar," he said.

"Who knows who you might be so quick to comfort next time," she said, and turned her back to him. "And I take back what I said," she tossed over her shoulder.

"About what?" he asked.

"About staying together awhile when this is over."

"If that's how you feel," he said. "Good night."

She made a small sound and he turned on his side and slept. He'd not be reaching her with sweet words or glib excuses, he knew, and perhaps it was just as well.

When the morning dawned and he rose, he felt his strength had almost fully returned and he had no further dizzy spells. He picked up the lone set of hoofprints that were Julie's horse's, and Denise rode beside him as he followed the trail. She had gone east, following a narrow, rock-lined passage that led down from the highland. By the time the day came to a close, she had left the dry harsh terrain of the Mesabi Range. The terrain grew softer, the black walnut more plentiful.

When night descended again, Fargo halted in a small arbor. "She's not been wandering about," he said to Denise. "She knows where she's going. But we'll catch her tomorrow."

"Good," Denise said. She undressed, lay down on her blanket, quickly fell asleep without any further words. She woke early as he did, and dressed in silence. Fargo then led the way across low, rolling hills with heavy tree cover. By midday, the air had turned sharply cooler and a mist coated the lowland as Fargo followed Julie's trail deeper into forest land. She had turned northeast, he saw.

"She's heading for the Canadian border, I'd guess," Fargo said. "But she's in no hurry, riding slow and easy."

The air continued to grow cooler and blanket the still-warm ground and the mists grew heavier. By mid-afternoon they formed a steady and slow-moving haze blanket over most of the land. He had to stop often to search the ground on foot for the hoofmarks and it was growing late in the day when he heard the roar of a waterfall. Julie's trail led toward the sound, which quickly grew louder.

"No little woodland waterfall," Fargo said. "This is a big one." Denise nodded and he cast a sharp glance at her. "The closer we get to her, the more sullen you become. What's in your craw, girl?"

"Nothing," she snapped. "I just want to get it over with."

"That makes two of us," he tossed back, spurring the pinto forward. A break in the mist showed the hoofprints leading up a hill and then down a narrow deer trail in the woods. The waterfall was a roaring sound now, so close he could feel its dampness in the air. The deer trail suddenly veered downward to the left, but he saw the hoofprints leave it and cut through the trees. He followed and reined to a halt where the trees ended. The roaring waterfall cascaded downward directly in front of him, not more than fifty yards away, and in front of it, on a cleared flat ledge of land, he saw a small cabin. A thin plume of gray smoke rose from the chimney. The door hung open and two horses were tethered to a tree nearby, one of them Julie's.

He caught Denise's quick, frowning glance and he shrugged and slid from the saddle. The long shadows were moving down the hill, and the mist that lay carpeting the ground began to grow thicker. When dusk came, it would build to a heavy fog, he knew. His eyes went to the enormous waterfall that hurled itself down just beyond the ledge with awesome beauty and frightening force. At the cabin he caught movement in the doorway and Julie stepped out, one arm around the waist of a tall man with curly black hair and a handsome, boyish face. He carried a small ax and they halted at the trees and began to chop low branches for firewood. But not before Julie gave him a long, lingering kiss.

"I'll be damned," Denise breathed. "Little Miss Goodness has had a boyfriend stashed away up here all the time."

"Seems that way," Fargo said as Julie gathered up the cut firewood and carried it to the house, her firm rear rolling inside riding britches. She came back outside in a few moments to wrap herself around the man as they walked back to the cabin.

"Found some wild onions for the stew," the man said.

"You're a gem, Chuck." Julie laughed and hugged him tighter as they disappeared inside the cabin.

"The little bitch," Denise hissed. "She murdered two people, three at her count, and she's carrying on as if nothing had happened."

"I've seen that often enough in the past. A conscience is something some people just don't have," Fargo said.

"You think Handsome Chuck had anything to do with what happened. Was he in on it?" Denise asked.

Fargo cast a quick, sly glance at her. "You're the one with all the female intuition. What do you think?"

Denise's eyes narrowed in thought as she stared at the cabin. "I'd say no," she answered. "She probably gave him the same bullshit story about Uncle Cyrus and Tom Colson both wanting to help her."

"You acting on reasons or a gut feeling?" Fargo smiled.

"Gut feeling, of course," Denise shot back, and he laughed softly.

"I go along with you," Fargo said. "She'd no reason to tell him anything differently. That makes Chuck a little bit of a problem."

"How?" Denise asked.

"He has no blame in anything. I don't want to kill him," Fargo said. "But that's what'll happen if I barge in. He'll come flying to her rescue."

"So what do we do?" Denise asked.

"I figure out a way to get past him to Julie," Fargo said.

Denise dismounted to sit down nearby as, on one knee, Fargo watched the last of the day slide into twilight. The fog began to roll down from the hills, beckoned by the warm earth, the perfect mixture of warmth, coolness, and dampness fueling nature's kettle. When night came, the little cabin was obscured by the fog, only the faint, diffuse orange glow of lamplight from inside showing through the gray-white veil that shrouded the hills. But the rushing, hissing sound of the waterfall seemed even louder in the darkness.

Fargo finally rose and Denise got up at once also. "Thought of a plan?" she asked.

He nodded, his jaw set. "First part's being a Peeping Tom. Second part depends on what I see."

"And I just stay here and wait," she sniffed.

"Wouldn't think of it," Fargo said. "Give me fifteen minutes and then take my lariat and come after me. Just head for the light, same as I'm going to do. If it goes out, you won't be able to see. You turn around and come back here, understand?" She made a face but nodded. "You'll never see the ledge by the waterfall in this fog. You'll go right over."

He turned from her and hurried from the trees, enshrouded in the thick fog at once. Using the orange glow of the light as a beacon, he headed toward it, watched it grow stronger, and finally saw the cabin. It appeared ghostlike in the fog that swirled around it. The glow of lamplight came from the lone window. In a crouch, he crossed the last few feet to the window and peered inside. The cabin was one large room with a hearth at one end, mattresses at the other. The kerosene lamp burned brightly on full beside the mattress and he saw Julie taking off her last garment, a pink pair of bloomers. Chuck was already undressed, he saw, and he watched as Julie lay back on the mattress, her legs stretched out.

"Come on, Chuck, honey," she murmured. "I don't like waiting."

Little Miss Goodness was nowhere around, Fargo mused.

Chuck hurried to the mattress and lowered himself over the round, compact figure. Julie's arm reached out and she turned the lamp off to plunge the room in darkness. But her moans of pleasure began almost at once, and Fargo turned from the window for a moment while a grim smile edged his lips. Julie Hudson deserved something more than just being caught, he mused. She deserved something to last forever in her scheming, murderous mind.

He glanced out into the fog, listened, and heard nothing. The light had gone out quickly, long before Denise was due to reach him. He could only hope she'd obey his orders. But he had other things to think about now, he told himself as he removed his gun belt, then began to pull off clothes.

When he was naked, he picked up the Colt and edged toward the open door of the cabin. Julie's moans had increased now and he halted at the doorway and drew the butt of the Colt across the side of the cabin. It made a series of bumping, scraping sounds.

"What was that?" he heard Chuck say inside the cabin.

"Nothing . . . mmmm . . . forget it," Julie murmured, but Fargo drew the Colt across the logs again, harder this time.

"Something's out there," Chuck said.

Fargo struck the gun butt hard against the outer wall, three sharp rapping sounds.

"Nothing," Julie murmured.

"Nothing, hell. I'm going to see," Chuck said, and Fargo heard Julie's little hiss of angry protest.

The Trailsman flattened himself against the outer wall of the cabin at the edge of the door, heard the man approaching, and then Chuck stepped outside, a rifle in his hands, his gaze straining out into the fog. Fargo brought the butt of the heavy Colt down in a sharp, short arc and caught the man as he collapsed. He pulled the figure from near the door and dropped it on the ground beside the cabin. On soft, barefoot steps, Fargo slipped in through the cabin door.

"I told you it was nothing," Julie said from the mattress, a disembodied voice. "Come to me, dammit."

Fargo let his lips form a muffled response and he moved to the mattress, Julie's body a dim white form in front of him. He lowered himself to the mattress, came over her, and her arms reached out, encircled his neck. Her legs spread out, knees lifting, and Fargo felt himself erect, desire fed by the power of anger, sudden passion made of pure domination, the desire to strike out, not to please. She was waiting, offering, and he pushed into her, a hard, driving thrust. "Oh, God, aaaah," Julie gasped as he drew back and thrust again. "Oh, yes . . . aaaiiieee," Julie cried out and cried out again as he thrust back and forth.

He reached over with one hand, found the kerosene lamp, and turned it up. He saw Julie's eyes come open, blink, stare at him, and he waited, stayed inside her. Her round blue eyes began to widen and grow dark as something more than horror, something beyond terror, rose up inside them. Her lips drew back, her jaw dropping, but it was the stark, unworldly light in her eyes that fascinated him. Her scream seemed a slow sound, but it was a tearing, shattering cry in reality. It shook the little cabin walls, circled in the air, and came again, shorter but no less shattering. She flung herself back, heels digging into the mattress, pulled from his pulsating organ.

"No. No, you're dead," Julie screamed. "You're dead. No-o-o-ooooooo."

"It's me, Chuck," Fargo said, and Julie flung herself against the wall, pushed to her feet. "Chuck," he said again as he moved toward her.

"My God, no, no . . . oh, Jesus," she screamed, her face contorted as she stared at him.

He reached an arm toward her slowly. "Who am I?" he asked.

She ducked away from him and, half bent over, ran past him, the high, round breasts jiggling only slightly.

"Don't you know who I am? It's Chuck," he called.

"No, you're not Chuck. Oh, God . . . oh, God," she screamed, the shock and terror still stark in her face. She ran toward the door and he sprang after her, saw her cast a glance back at him with monstrous fear. He ran toward her, both arms outstretched, and saw her disappear into the fog outside. He dropped his arms and raced from the cabin, halted, his lips pulled back.

"No, no, oh, God, no," he heard her gasping as she ran and then, abruptly, the gasped cries became a terrible, spiraling wail of finality. He stopped in his tracks and listened to Julie Hudson's last crying scream mingle with the rushing hiss of the waterfall, trail away, and finally end in nothingness.

He turned slowly and moved back to the glow of light that was the cabin. It was over, not precisely as he'd planned the final moment, but it was over. Perhaps the best way, after all, he mused as he reached the cabin and began to pull on clothes. He'd just finished dressing when he saw the figure materialize through the fog. He waited, hand on his gun, until Denise came into definition.

"I saw the light go off just as I was halfway down. I turned around, as you told me to," she said. "But when I saw it go on again, I decided to come down." She looked at the still-unconscious form of the man on the ground. "I heard her scream," she said, her lips tightening. "She was running from you."

"She was running from ghosts," he answered. "From ghosts outside and inside, you might say." He turned and strode into the cabin and Denise followed. He pointed to where the small pile of sacks rested in one corner. "Take one," he said. "Take them all if you like."

"No, I don't want it. Too much blood on it. I'll take enough to cover what I'm owed," Denise said, and he waited as she opened one sack and counted out the silver pieces. She followed him from the cabin. "What happens to the rest?" she asked.

"Chuck here can have it when he wakes up. He'll be a lucky man," Fargo said.

"Luckier than he knows," Denise added, and hurried after Fargo as he made his way through the fog to where he'd left the horses. He climbed into the saddle, led the way back into the hills until he was far enough away from the waterfall not to hear it any longer. He found a place to bed down and drew his own sigh of relief as he stretched out.

Denise stayed on her blanket and Fargo let his eyes close, aware of the bitter taste inside his mouth that only time would dissipate.

He slept soundly and the morning brought a bright sun and a cool breeze that quickly shredded the fog and mists. He found a stream, washed, and let Denise do the same. "I'll drop you off someplace safe and it's safe riding for you from there," he said.

She tossed him a half-pout. "No! You said we'd spend a while together when it was over."

"You said you took that back." He frowned.

"I take back what I took back," she snapped impatiently.

"Prove it," he said, and her mouth was on his at once, devouring, sweet-firm lips working hungrily.

"Will that do?" she asked.

"For now." He grinned, patted her rear, and lifted her onto her horse.

The lake-filled Minnesota land was a place fit for loving and forgetting, and he knew he'd do both. For a while.

*The Kentucky-Tennessee border, 1859,
south of Boone's Trace and the Cumberland gap,
a cradle of savage history where today
was never far from yesterday . . .*

The girl had asked to ride along with him. Amy Powell had a fresh, scrubbed, open-faced prettiness to her,
she was part of the wagon train, and he'd no reason to
say no to her. Until now.

"Canyon O'Grady, that's an unusual name," the
girl said. Her appraising stare took in the big man,
well over six feet, with a shock of flame-red hair,
crackling blue eyes in a roguish face, and a lilt to his
speech.

"It is that and I'm an unusual fellow." Canyon

O'Grady smiled, but his eyes narrowed as they swept the line of white ash beyond her in the light that was almost dusk. "You get down to the wagons, now, lass," he muttered.

"Why?" Amy Powell frowned in protest.

His eyes stayed on the line of trees. "There's a time for doing and a time for asking. This is a time for doing," he said sharply. "Get your little ass back to the wagons and tell Alex Koosman to make camp in that glen up ahead. I'll be along later."

She hesitated, but saw the sternness in his usually roguish face. She quickly sent her horse down toward the five wagons rolling along the old antelope trail below. Canyon O'Grady returned his crackling blue eyes to the deep stand of white ash. They were still there, the silent, wraithlike horsemen moving through the trees. They had seen him, of course, decided he was unimportant to their eventual plans and continued to parallel the wagons below. Their nearly naked bodies and saddleless freedom were a mask for their perfect discipline. Probably Shawnee, he guessed. His hand stroked the neck of the magnificent palomino he rode, its coppery sheen glistening in the last of the sunlight. He watched the silent forms move on through the trees.

There were men, women, and children in that wagon train he guided, a sufficient reason to do his damnedest to protect it. But in addition, he had his own special reasons, the same ones that had brought him to hire on as an outrider. He turned the palomino into the trees, but hung back far enough to be unseen. The Indians were watching the wagons below, and they'd see the camp made in the glen as dusk began to throw its lavender shawl across the low mountain country. The braves would camp also, he was certain. Night attacks were not favored by most Indians.

As dusk grew darker, O'Grady continued to hang back, though he still followed. The Indian band would rest overnight and use the fresh morning light to make their attack. As the dusk turned into night O'Grady finally halted, slipped from the saddle, and threw the palomino's reins over a low branch. He waited, sank to one knee, and when the moon began to filter through the trees, he moved forward on foot, testing each step.

The pale half moon gave precious little light through the thick foliage, and Canyon O'Grady relied on his nose as he crept forward. His nostrils flared as he drew in deep breaths and sought the unmistakable, musky odor of damp coonskin and bear grease. Suddenly, as his nose caught the smells, he halted and sank to a crouch as he moved forward again. He moved in quick bursts from one tree to another, his eyes searching the darkness, and he finally came to a halt again. They had bedded down with no campfire, and O'Grady used the pale moonlight to count the figures that lay on the ground in a ragged circle. When he finished, he moved backward with the silence of a diamond-backed water snake in a pond. He returned to the palomino and walked the horse down the slope to the passage at the bottom, where he swung into the saddle again. He rode the half mile forward to the half circle of the wagons, three Conestogas, and two big Bucks County hay wagons outfitted with canvas tops.

He entered the half circle and dismounted. Supper had just ended, but one of the women handed him a plate with a chicken leg and beans. He felt the eyes focused on him as he spoke to Alex Koosman, the wagonmaster. "You've company," he said between bites. "Damn near twenty of them by my count."

O'Grady saw the alarm take instant hold in Alex Koosman's broad, lined face. He was a large man, well on in years but still strong and his hair still had a blond tone under the gray. He sported heavy leather suspenders. "We'll have to prepare to defend ourselves come morning," he said gravely.

"You'll have to do more than that," Canyon said and saw the question come into Alex Koosman's eyes. "You can't let them attack full force. You'll never stand up to it."

"What else can we do?" the wagonmaster asked.

"Hit them first. Cut them down before they attack," Canyon said. "I'll want ten men ready to go an hour before dawn."

"I'll pick them out myself," Koosman said.

"The others stay here to defend the wagons in case you still get an attack," Canyon ordered. "Meanwhile, I'll get some sleep. Have your men do the same. I want them rested and able to shoot straight." He led the palomino to one side of the camp and sat down against the trunk of a box elder and watched Koosman gather his men together. When Koosman finished, he returned to his Conestoga and Canyon's lips pursed. He wouldn't take Koosman with him. He wanted the man here in the relative safety of the wagons. That was important, Canyon murmured to himself as he leaned his head back against the tree and watched Amy Powell come by. She halted, her gaze appraising him again.

"I still want to learn more about Canyon O'Grady," she said.

"Another time, another place, lass," he told her and she walked away, her trim little rear a joy to watch. The camp grew still finally, and he closed his eyes and slept soundly until, with the unfailing, instinctual clock inside him, he woke and saw the half moon at the far end of the sky. He stood, checked the big Army Colt with the ivory grips, and waited as the ten men emerged from their wagons, Alex Koosman one of them. "You stay here with the wagons," Canyon said. "They'll need you if the Shawnee attack."

Koosman obliged and Canyon motioned for the others to follow him as he swung onto the palomino. They filed in behind him as he started up the dark slope, and he led them halfway to the top before he dismounted, gesturing for the men to leave their horses in the thick brush and follow him on foot. He moved uphill again and finally halted. He let the others gather around him. Most were young men, he saw, their faces more determined than grave. "They'll hear us if we try to get any closer," he said. "Spread out on both sides of the hill. They'll be coming down between us. When I fire the first shot, pour it into them. If we can cut them in half we've saved the wagons, even if the rest of them still attack."

The men nodded and spread out on both sides of the hill. Canyon settled down in the trees and stayed motionless. As the first gray light of dawn trickled down through the heavily wooded slope Canyon noted that the others had done a good job of vanishing into the trees. He drew the big Colt as the gray grew lighter and the woods took shape. His hand closed around the ivory grips as he spotted the horsemen slowly moving down the slope. They moved unhurriedly, riding in clusters of two and three except for the one in the lead, a moon-faced brave with a short torso and thin legs. Canyon's eyes went to the markings on the brow band the Indian wore. He had guessed right. Shawnee.

He let the Indian pass, move on some dozen feet while those following came to the center of the slope. He half rose, took aim, and fired. The first Shawnee flew from his pony in a tangle of flailing arms and legs. The hillside erupted in gunfire. Canyon dropped low as a half-dozen stray bullets smashed into the trees around him. He peered through the leaves and saw the Shawnee wheeling in confusion as they were cut down by the withering cross fire. He paused to take aim again and fire and another of the Indians toppled backward over the rump of his pony. But the Shawnee who had escaped the cross fire had sent their ponies racing downhill, determined to strike at the wagon train and salvage some measure of victory, something to bring back to the council fires to avoid complete defeat.

"Get to your horses," Canyon shouted at the men who had mostly broken off firing. He began to run headlong down the slope. A quick glance backward showed at least eight slain Shawnee littering the hillside, and when he spotted the palomino, he vaulted into the saddle without breaking stride, the shock of red hair tossed like living flame. He sent the horse streaking downhill toward the gunfire from below which was interspersed with high-pitched, whooping cries.

The wagons and their attackers came into sight in moments, the Shawnees making back-and-forth sweeps in front of the wagons, firing both bows and arrows and rifles. Cut down to less than half their strength, they poured arrows and bullets into the wagons more out of frustrated fury than a serious attempt to storm the half circle of defenders.

Canyon streaked into open land, aimed, and one of the Shawnee cried out as he fell from his horse. The other men were racing into the open behind him now, and the remaining Shawnee wheeled their ponies and broke off the attack on the wagons, unwilling to be caught again in a cross fire. They streaked off in all directions as they fled into the trees.

Canyon pulled the palomino to a halt. Pursuit would be pointless, he realized, and he turned to the wagons with a frown. The Shawnee had poured a lot of fury into the half circle of wagons. Stray bullets and stray arrows could kill as thoroughly as well-aimed ones, and he felt a stab of relief course through him when Alex Koosman came out from behind his Conestoga.

"Anybody hurt?" Canyon questioned.

"Tom Skew took a bullet in the side, Abe Husack got himself a scraped temple, and Hilda Powell caught an arrow in the leg," Alex Koosman said.

"Hilda Powell, Amy's mother?" Canyon frowned.

"That's right. We can reach Pickett in three hours if we can leave. They can hold out till then, but any longer might be risky. Infection's sure to set in," the man said.

"You can roll," Canyon told him. "There won't be any more trouble from that bunch. They've gone off to get their dead and lick their wounds." Alex Koosman nodded and hurried off to get the wagons started. Canyon saw a small knot of figures around the second Conestoga, where Amy looked on nervously. He strolled over and the girl's eyes went to him. "We'll get her to Pickett. There'll be a doc there," he said reassuringly.

"I hear that if it hadn't been for you, we might all be dead," Amy said.

"That's about true," Canyon said.

Amusement touched the girl's eyes. "I see you don't believe in modesty," she said.

"Modesty's a vice, not a virtue," Canyon said. "It's for those who need it."

"I still want to know more about Canyon O'Grady."

"Maybe, when we get to Pickett. Go see to your ma now," Canyon said. He strode to Alex Koosman, who had begun to lead the lead wagon out of the glen. Canyon stood by and watched the five wagons move out. He returned the waves of those on the wagons and wished he'd tried harder to remember their names when he'd been introduced. But it hadn't mattered then and it didn't really matter now. Only Alex Koosman mattered.

Canyon swung onto the palomino and watched Koosman drive his Conestoga, concentration evident in his square, steady, salt-of-the-earth countenance. Maybe the years could give that to a man, he speculated.

O'Grady spurred the palomino forward to ride on ahead of the wagons. His eyes swept the full countryside, ripe with forests and rich land. In the distance the towering peaks of the Appalachians rose in purple-gray majesty. This was a land steeped in the history of the American nation, a spawning place for legends such as Daniel Boone and other fighting pioneers who had opened the land westward.

But it was not a land left behind by history's march. In this fertile region, yesterday was today, a place where all the tensions of men's ambitions and men's differences pulsated with living fervor. From below the Kentucky-Tennessee border came talk and rumours of a separate nation, a Confederacy of States, and from the north came talk of a new leader and a crusade to abolish slavery. But these were all still distant clouds that could blow away, he recognized, yet the passions and fears of men, the poor and the powerful, were stirred. It all added to the ferment in the land, to the everyday dangers of highway men and bandits, hostile Indians and horse thieves, four-legged as well as two-legged predators.

But danger was in his blood. Canyon O'Grady half smiled. Pursuit and death were handmaidens of his birth, truth and justice a flame that burned inside him. And this was his land now, this wild and mostly lawless America, and he had brought his gifts to offer those who cared about right and wrong, truth and honor. It was a grim smile that stayed on his lips as he moved forward, his crackling blue eyes searching the terrain until he found a place where the old antelope trail neared a proper road. He halted, waited for the wagons to come into sight, waved them forward, and waited again until they reached the road. "Stay on it," he called back. He put the palomino into a gallop and soon saw that the road wound its way into Pickett. He rode into the bustling town, asked for and found the doctor, and had the man waiting when the wagons arrived.

While the wounded were helped into the doctor's house, Canyon rode through Pickett and found it to be pretty much the same as most towns, a little neater than the sprawling towns of the Plains country, but with enough rowdy and ragged characters of its own. He saw Studebaker seed wagons, plenty of Owensboro Mountain wagons with their oversized brakes, and an assortment of buckboards and surreys. Pioneers and mountain men passed through Pickett, but he saw enough small, neat houses to show that the town held a substantial number of good citizens. Further proof was the fact that beside the saloon and dance hall in the center of town, he saw a proper church amid the usual general store and barber shop.

When he finished sizing up the town, he returned to the doctor's house and was told the wagons had camped beyond the west end of town. He found them there, drawn up on a loose half circle, and Alex Koosman hurried forward as the big redheaded man rode up. "The doc wants to keep everyone for a few days to see how they're healing before we go on," Alex said.

"That's wise," Canyon replied.

"I've a niece here in Pickett, Adeline Koosman, a lot younger than I am," the wagonmaster said. "I wrote her I'd stop by when we passed through. Now I'll have a little more time to spend with her. But first, I want to buy you a drink, Canyon O'Grady."

"My father taught me never to refuse a good drink or a warm woman," Canyon said. "I've abided by that ever since."

"Good. Tom Wideman and Frank Strawser asked to come along. The whole wagon train's beholden to you, Canyon," the man said. "I'll be right back." Canyon nodded and the wagonmaster soon reappeared on his horse, the two men riding alongside him. Canyon swung in beside the trio and saw Amy Powell watching him from her Conestoga. She offered a small nod as he passed, and he made a mental note to pay more attention to the girl when he returned. She was more than a little curious about him and he liked a curious woman. Curiosity was a powerful force that often carried over into the bedroom.

Alex Koosman's voice broke into his pleasant anticipation as the men reined up in front of the saloon. "It'll be my pleasure, gents," Koosman said and led the way into the saloon.

Canyon took in the big room, already beginning to fill with customers though it was hardly past midday. A bar filled one wall with some dozen customers there, and Alex motioned everyone to one of the round tables. A young woman came to take their order, her face once pretty but now merely empty. "Whiskey," Canyon ordered and hoped it wouldn't be too undrinkable. Wideman and Strawser ordered the same and Alex Koosman a beer.

"After we left the doctor, I took a minute to stop in

and see my niece," Koosman said. "Haven't seen Adeline in ten years. It's going to be nice to have a long visit with her tomorrow."

"None of us might be here if it weren't for Canyon," Tom Wideman said as the girl returned with their drinks.

"Indeed, it was a lucky day when you showed up to sign on as outrider for us, Canyon O'Grady," Alex Koosman agreed, and he raised his stein of beer in a toast. Canyon took a sip of the whiskey and was grateful to find it strong and rich. He had just taken another sip when he saw four men as they came into the saloon.

The hairs on the back of his neck suddenly grew stiff. They spelled trouble, he knew at once, partly from instinct, partly from experience, and partly from observation. All four had hard, nervous faces and darting eyes, their hands resting on the butts of their six-guns. One with a Stetson with a tear in the brim walked a half step ahead of the others as they started toward the bar. But he saw their eyes sweep the room in quick but all-seeing glances.

Trouble, Canyon thought again, yet he wasn't prepared for it to erupt the way it did. The four men were almost at the bar when they whirled, almost as one, drawing their six-guns as they did. They poured bullets directly into Alex Koosman. . . .

LOOKING FORWARD!

**The following is the opening
section from the next novel in the exciting
Trailsman series from Signet:**

THE TRAILSMAN #91
CAVE OF DEATH

*July 1862, along the Arkansas River.
Once this was the headquarters of an empire,
but now the stench of decay masks
the odor of greed and savagery . . .*

Half a dozen men were wolfing down supper in the dining room of the stage station, but Senora Maria Teresa Espinoza y Vigil sat by herself. Her dark eyes sent unmistakable signals to only one—the tall, broad-shouldered man with shoulder-length black hair, a full beard, and lake-blue eyes which returned the senora's provocative messages. Skye Fargo had just stopped in for a sit-down meal during a trek from Santa Fe to Denver, and he got the distinct impression that the lady was in a hurry. After finishing her dinner, she wasted no time as she sidled past him and whispered that he'd be a welcome visitor to her room.

Less than a hour later, the cotton chemise, aided by

the Trailsman's nimble and eager fingers, dropped from Senora Vigil's rounded shoulders. The plump but appealing woman sighed and stepped back a bit, giving Fargo a better view of her full breasts.

He had never seen a pair he didn't like, and hers looked damn good in this soft glow. The flickering and smoky tallow candle sat atop an iron holder that had been jammed into the adobe wall. Her tiny room, perhaps eight feet square, sat at a stage stop on the north bank of the Arkansas River, about seventy miles east of the Rocky Mountains.

The stage stop was still called Bent's Old Fort, in honor of William and Charles Bent, who had built it back in 1833. These days, however, much of the immense adobe castle was just ruins, melting back into the earth. What remained were a few sleeping rooms on each side of the old main gate, a kitchen and dining room, a smithy, and facilities for a few dozen mules, which outnumbered the people here by a considerable margin. But Jared Sanderson, the local manager for the Kansas City, Santa Fe & Canon City Fast Line, was trying hard—Senora Vigil's room had a fresh coat of whitewash.

Senora Vigil seemed to think she could use a fresh coat of paint too, and she stepped back a bit. She pouted pensively while the Trailsman's eyes sparkled and his generally serious expression lifted into the start of an appreciative grin. But that wasn't enough to improve her disposition.

"Alas," the short and roundish woman murmured, "the passing years are not as kind to women as they are to men."

Those candlelit highlights in her shoulder-length, raven-black hair might well have been small streaks of gray, perhaps her midsection had been a little flatter a few years ago, and maybe those luscious breasts did sag a bit, but Fargo didn't see any cause for complaint.

"No," he soothed, "beautiful women are like fine wine—they just get better with age." He was sure he'd said the right thing when her fingers returned to removing his shirt.

"It was most kind of you to say that, Senor, even though you cannot really believe such a thing," she whispered while the Trailsman bent down, first cupping her breasts, then nuzzling her nipples until they grew to be as large as, and considerably sweeter than, the chokecherries that grew along the river.

Senora Vigil sighed contentedly. Her strong hands began to knead the Trailsman's shoulder blades. He eased his own hands down the hollow of her back to the top of her frilly drawers. He slid one hand below to savor the swell of her firm rump.

She sighed again, but then shook her head. A bit of determination crept into her round face, and she backed up so that one more step would put her atop the bed.

It wasn't the normal bed that had a frame. It was more of a bench, made in a hollow of the thick adobe outer wall. A cornhusk mattress provided some comfort, and gaudy Navaho trade blankets served as the covers—which were hardly necessary on this August night. The room was sweltering, and Fargo felt even hotter, even though Senora Vigil now seemed intent on cooling things.

"Oh, Senor, what kind of woman do you take me for?" she teased.

"One who knows a good thing when she sees it," Fargo muttered, not really of a mind to talk. Getting his hands back under those drawers seemed a lot more important than any of this foolish chatter.

She batted her long, dark lashes as Fargo straightened and pressed tight against her, just so she'd know that she had inspired a throbbing insistence that was growing by the minute.

"That is true, Senor," she conceded, her voice husky. "But I am not a woman of haste."

During dinner Fargo had listened halfheartedly to the woman's story of woe. It was a commonplace tale of petty complaints about the dusty and jarring stage ride that she had endured. Her lamentation ended with her abandonment at this stage station. Apparently, her man hadn't met her stage as planned. He was supposed to get her to their land, a hundred miles to the west, but whoever he was, he hadn't shown up by dinner, which meant he wasn't likely to appear before morning.

Although Fargo hadn't been attracted by the woman's petulant whine, he couldn't make himself ignore the rise and fall of her heavy bosom when she sighed out her story. The Trailsman felt a surge of irritation as he recalled how hastily she had cajoled him to her room. He'd barely managed to finish dinner. And now she was saying that she wanted to take things slow and easy.

Well, as long as a man was enjoying what he was doing, there wasn't any cause for undue haste. Fargo took a deep breath of heat and tallow smoke. He slid his hands back around, staying atop those silk underthings this time. Through the smooth silk he pressed and rubbed her jutting buttocks, which soon began a rhythmic motion of their own.

Before long, Senora Vigil didn't mind that Fargo's probing hands were beneath the silk. So that she could pretend she didn't know what was going on, he proceeded slowly. His hands slid round to the outermost swell of her hips. He bowed his wrists so that the drawers slid down, then eased down and repeated the process until her most interesting parts were within reach.

Out in the hard-packed yard under a rising full moon, some horses, along with a wagon or two, drew up amid the furious barking of the resident mongrels. Wafting in through the room's tiny window, the commotion inspired Senora Vigil to move a little faster. Her fingers found the buttons of Fargo's fly. In what seemed but an instant, the Trailsman was stepping out of his denim trousers.

With his patient help, her drawers had slipped down near her knees by that time. Embracing him tightly about the waist, as his shaft prodded against her soft navel, Senora Vigil danced back. After confirming that the bed was right behind her, she lay back, pulling the Trailsman down atop her.

Now she was in a hurry. Her breath came in feverish gasps. She moved her hands down, as if to push him into her as her thighs spread wide and began to envelop him.

Fargo didn't need much encouragement. He plunged into her welcome moistness, pressing down as she arched up to meet him. Her bare feet, still planted on the woven mat next to the bed's niche, gave her enough leverage to insure that their initial coupling was deep and complete.

That tremendous thrust was more than Senora Vigil had planned on. "You are too much for me, Senor," she protested, the words tumbling out in a frenzied mixture of English and Spanish.

Fargo knew better, as did the rest of her body, so he smothered further protests with a kiss, and continued to thrust. She sidled, so as to get her feet off the floor, and Fargo went along with it. They were both atop the blankets, pounding away, when she started to shudder.

Her ankles locked over the Trailsman, and her plump thighs squeezed his hips with a bear-trap grip. Her hands rained little hammerlike blows on his back.

Fargo slid his hands off her shoulders, pressing them against the bed so he could lift his torso and slide into a more comfortable position—this bed had a wall at each end, and it had been built for shorter people.

Before settling back down, he enjoyed the view of her dark-eyed passion. Her rolling and heaving huge breasts were flushed from pressing against him. Her hips rose and fell, then rose again to grasp his submerged organ more tightly.

"Now, Senor, now," she urged. "Wait no longer."

The Trailsman didn't argue with her, but he didn't rush to cooperate, either. He settled back down against her so that every possible bit of her eager flesh was pressed against his. It was just what a man needed after a lonely week in the saddle, bound for no particular place.

What a man didn't need right now was an interruption, but one was coming. Fargo's sensitive ears heard padding footsteps outside, their sound barely audible above Maria's purr. He rolled across her, getting to his gun just as the door was kicked open, its flimsy latch flying across the room.

The angry man standing in the portal was dressed vaquero-style—polished boots with high heels and narrow toes, tight black twill trousers with some silver along the outer seams, a loose white cotton shirt with embroidered patterns, and a tremendous dark sombrero. His extensive mustache bristled and his eyes flashed in anger, which was something to consider, since he had a cocked revolver in his right hand.

"Unhand my wife, you gringo bastard," he announced.

"As you can see," Fargo replied from his naked

crouch on the floor, "I don't have a hand, or anything else, on that woman."

When the man shifted his glare to confirm that, Fargo used the opportunity to silently bring up his own pistol. He kept it close to his right side, in the shade of his body where it wouldn't be seen.

"You have shamed me and destroyed my honor, Senor," the intruder proclaimed. His voice dropped into a more polished baritone. "I, Ramon, her lawful husband—I demand satisfaction."

This wasn't the first time the Trailsman had been caught in the old badger game. Every footloose man got trapped occasionally, unless he was celibate.

A woman would act real available. Then she'd make it clear that her man wasn't around. You'd get to her room, she'd shed a few clothes, but before the fun started in earnest, her partner—sometimes, but not necessarily, her husband—would appear. He'd brandish a pistol and wail about his sullied honor. After he made his speech, he'd get around to settling for all the money you had on you.

If this had been the usual badger game, Fargo would have caught on instantly. But Maria and Ramon were working it with some new variations. Maria had been so caustic in her complaining that it was hard to believe she was experienced at luring men. If Fargo hadn't just been alone on a trail for a week, her whining would have chased him away. As the game was usually played, Ramon should have shown up just in time to save his and Maria's "honor."

Ramon must have been delayed tonight, or else Maria had been more eager than usual. Fargo sometimes had that effect on women.

Ramon's low voice interrupted Fargo's thoughts. "Senor, did you not hear me? I demand satisfaction."

"You want a duel? How about here and now?"

Ramon blanched at the speed with which a long-barreled Colt revolver materialized from the shaded side of the Trailsman.

"Senor, perhaps there is a more sensible way to settle this outrage against my honor."

"Meaning that if I gave you a few double-eagles, your honor would be satisfied?"

Ramon nodded.

"That's too much," Fargo protested. "A plugged nickel would be too much for your honor. You're nothing but a worthless pimp. Your woman does all the work, and then you come around and do all the collecting. Couldn't you folks just be honest about what you're doing, and announce the price up front?"

Before Ramon could protest, Fargo rose, gun aimed at the man's sweat-soaked forehead. "You're going to drop that gun and sit on the bed with Maria until I'm out of here. Since it's too late to travel on tonight, I'm going to put on my duds and go find another room."

"But, Senor, you have shamed me, and I am a man of reputation," Ramon sputtered.

"Nobody will hear about this from me," Fargo promised.

Ramon slowly eased his gun back into its tooled-leather holster. "Senor, I ride here with my men, who are around here even now."

"You mean if I walk out of here all in one piece, they'll decide that you're a coward, and you'll lose your standing? Or else they'll decide that you're hurt, and they owe you some vengeance, so they'll take it out on me?"

Ramon nodded. "That is the situation, Senor. If you were to leave quietly some way, I could fire my pistol into this thick wall—then they would think all was in order."

"I think you're full of shit," Fargo proclaimed as he used his pistol to motion Ramon over to the bed, where Maria still sat in silence, tugging a blanket over her bosom even though she had nothing to hide from either man.

The Trailsman swapped his pistol from hand to hand as he tugged on his shirt. "You're bluffing, Ramon, and I'm calling your bluff. Your men are so busy getting drunk right now that they don't give a damn what happens to you." Ramon slumped, his arm across Maria's shoulders, as Fargo finished dressing and stomped out of the room.

Fargo had been right about Ramon's men. There were four of them, all dressed pretty much like their boss, although their clothes weren't quite so good. They sat at a wooden table in the dining room, which turned into a saloon after supper. They passed around a bottle of mescal. From the sound of their Spanish, they were bragging a lot about various women they had known. Two of them, though, had notably fair complexions, and they had to think a bit before they added their boasts to the conversation.

At the next table were three men passing around a jug of corn liquor, and bragging in slurred English. At the other table sat one man alone, who was nursing a stiff shot of bourbon. Gray-bearded and shaggy, he was slim and limber, although he was getting up there in years. He was trying to look more relaxed than he really was. Fargo knew him.

It wasn't polite to hail men like that by name, however, because they may have changed names recently. So the Trailsman stepped closer and started with a question. "Can you tell me where to find Sanderson? I need to see him about a room and a bottle."

The man grunted before he looked up and recognized the Trailsman. "He'll be back shortly. Have a seat."

Fargo took the offer. "Mind if I call you Zeb?"

"Do as good as any, I reckon. You're still Skye Fargo?" He grinned, but there was no way the man could look happy with all those scars on his lined face.

The Trailsman nodded. "Yep. Just on my way from nowhere to no place, and thought I'd stop in here."

"Wondered where you came from. Didn't see you on the stage with them." He waved toward the three men with the corn liquor. Then he shook his head toward the mescal table. "And you didn't ride in with them neither."

Zeb Reynolds had been a free trapper in Taos long ago, back when there was a market for beaver pelts and Bent's Fort was a going concern. When that had petered out, he'd started doing pretty much what the Trailsman did. Despite his age, Zeb was one of the better wagon masters, and still good at finding trails, blazing routes, and the like.

"How's the stage these days?" Fargo teased. "Never thought you'd get so old that you'd rather ride the stage than your own good horse."

Reynolds turned and spat before answering. "Bah. Ain't that old. Just simpler this way to get to my next job."

"They ain't put you out to pasture yet?" Fargo asked.

"Shit no. Got me a good job with Uncle Sam. When the stage pulls out for Pueblo tomorrow, I'll be aboard. And when I get there, I'll go on the payroll."

He suddenly became quiet as Ramon entered the room. Ramon's eyes flashed at Fargo. The Trailsman's hand started for his gun, but then Ramon's mouth turned up a bit. His expression seemed to be asking whether Fargo had told anybody about their recent encounter in Maria's room. Fargo shook his head slightly. Ramon slowly nodded, looking more pleasant by the second, and went over to join his men.

Right on his heels was the station agent, Jared Sanderson, who wore muttonchop whiskers so long that they brushed his shoulders. Fargo called for a bottle of bourbon and told Sanderson he'd be needing a room. Sanderson winked, and muttered something under his breath about how Maria Vigil ought to be horsewhipped. Then he explained that he was booked solid for the night.

Zeb told Fargo he was welcome to his floor, then began bragging at length about his new job. The government was starting an official survey of the mountainous parts of the West. The survey crew had been working down around Santa Fe. After finishing there, they would move north.

Surveyors made maps, but when they started the job, they didn't necessarily know a whole lot about the territory. To keep from getting themselves lost, they hired guides who knew a given area.

"So for three dollars a day, plus bacon and beans and my very own government mule, I'll lead them fancy-pants surveyors around the mountains," Zeb boasted. "We'll go up the Arkansas a spell from the Pueblo, where I'm supposed to meet up with 'em this week. Then up the Hardscrabble, over to the Greenhorn, across the Sangres—"

"The old Taos Trapper's Trail," Fargo interjected. "Hell, a blind man wouldn't need a guide for that."

"Ain't just showing the way," Zeb continued. "You do some hunting for fresh meat, help tend the stock, and cook some. They bring a couple of their own strikers to help, but you still do a considerable amount of the chores so that they have time in the evening to draw their maps and write down what they saw and did that day.

"It's not all that adventuresome, like the old days," Zeb admitted. Seeming inclined to lapse into embroidered tales of bygone times, Zeb paused before casting a wistful smile toward Fargo. "But it's easy work at top pay," he concluded.

In the past, Zeb had enjoyed a reputation for taking audacious risks. For those in the know, Zeb Reynolds' youthful exploits made better lore than the tales about Jim Beckwourth or Old Bill Williams. The old-timer's braggadocio concerning his new job struck Fargo as sad.

"There's worse ways to spend a summer," Fargo agreed after swallowing two fingers' worth of wretched bourbon and passing the bottle to Zeb.

Zeb matched Fargo's swig and belched. "Indeed there are. And it's tolerable safe work, too. Redskins don't pester surveyors much, and the folks that're settled love to see the surveyors."

Most folks in the West didn't like to see anybody from the government, so Fargo asked why surveyors were an exception.

"I'm not a lawyer, so I can't tell you all of it. But the way I understand it, if you go off and squat somewhere and start raisin' corn or cows or whatever, you can't get a legal title to the land you're on till it's been surveyed. Then the government has a proper description of where your land ends and another man's starts. Most folks like the idea of owning their land fair and square, so the surveyors get a decent welcome."

The rest of the room must have been interested in government surveys, because as Zeb continued after pulling down some more bourbon, the other chatter